Desperate Journeys

**Five Suspenseful,
Action-Packed Crime Stories**

By Russ Towne

Editing: Karen M. Smith, Hen House Publishing
Cover Design: Karen M. Smith, Hen House Publishing
Interior Layout: Karen M. Smith, Hen House Publishing
Cover image courtesy of Eugene Triguba via Unsplash.com

ISBN 13: 978-1-948245-08-1

What readers are saying:

Blood Oaths

"So full of suspense it kept me on the edge of my seat. It's a wonderful tale of redemption and truth on so many levels."

"Wow what a read ... totally gripping.I read it very fast as it was too dangerous to stop."

No Choice

"A great suspenseful story with a gripping and satisfying ending."

The Misunderstanding

"Really scary. It makes me want a dog. Gruesome cowboy-style justice."

Desperate Journeys

"Absolutely terrifying. Suspense readers will love these stories."

The Patsy

"It gripped me from the very first and rolls seamlessly along."

"I like that the story was told with a fresh angle, from the con man's point of view."

Acknowledgments

Several people have helped to improve this book. Though I listen to and consider all feedback I receive from them, and often follow it, any errors or inconsistencies that remain are most likely the result of my not heeding their excellent advice.

Thank you to Karen M. Smith of Hen House Publishing for excellent editing and book design.

I also greatly appreciate the people who volunteered to suffer through reading the rough drafts and for providing excellent feedback and expertise regarding plot holes, contuinity issues, story flow, a variety of technical aspects, and much more:

Heidi Towne
Scott Harris
TM Blayte
Karen Stanford
Pamela Read
Beth Kennedy
Ute Lark

Thank you also to my:

Beloved wife, life partner, and friend: Heidi
Parents: Sam and Tricia Towne
Children: Ben, Brian, and Stephanie
Grandchildren: Thomas, Zachary, Alexander, Raiden, and Riley
In-laws: Bob and Jane Fakuda

You help make my life a great adventure.

I'm immensely grateful to all of you. Thank you! May your days be filled with blessings.

Love,

Russ

Introduction

This labor of love began years ago as five very short stories, also known as microfiction, that I'd written and published over the years. I kept hearing from readers who said they thought the ideas behind those tales had the potential to be full-blown stories or perhaps even their own novels. I agreed. Herein are the enhanced and expanded versions of those very short stories of long ago. May you find them worthy of your time.

To my brother Randy with love and respect.

Table of Contents

Desperate Journey

BLAM-BANG!

The explosions jerked me awake in the darkness of that warm summer night in 1970. Our vehicle wobbled wildly as if the top-heavy, metal beast were trying to decide whether to flip over sideways or topple end-over-end. It spun and bucked from side to side. A kaleidoscope of zigzagging lights streaked and bounced around us. Terrified, we screamed and grabbed for something to hang onto and braced for the inevitable crash or roll. Time seemed to slow to a crawl while our world spun out of control in a fast-motion nightmare.

When we finally stopped spinning, dual shock waves of blaring horns and glaring lights from two rapidly approaching eighteen-wheelers hit us, mixing with the sounds of our screams. With our heads still twirling we looked out the front windshield. It took a moment and a couple of blinks to clear my head and vision enough to see the two metal monsters roaring down on us as we straddled both lanes facing the wrong way on the freeway. Side-by-side, they barreled down the two northbound lanes, much too close to stop in time to miss us. I jerked my head down, squeezed my eyelids closed, and clenched every muscle in my body, knowing we'd all be dead in the next second or two. Our vehicle rocked violently as the trucks roared past so close on either side that it felt and sounded like twin tornadoes trying to tear us from the road.

We were shaking even after our vehicle finally stopped rocking. I sat on a bench seat, jammed between my mom and her friend Mary in the Red Beast. That's what I affectionately called my parent's International Harvester Travel-all, a large predecessor to SUVs. It had huge tires for off-roading in treacherous terrain. While great in dirt and mud, they raised the vehicle's center-of-gravity, making it top-heavy, especially with seven of us crammed into it. It was about 3:00 am and we were on a lonely stretch of Interstate 5 between small farming communities on our way to Disneyland.

In the driver's seat, Mary quickly came to her senses and eased our very wobbly, stricken Travelall to the shoulder of the freeway. The women hugged the youngest children and wiped their tears, making sure no one was hurt beyond some bumped noggins and knees. Mom told all the rest of the kids to stay in the Travelall, as she, Mary, and I got out to see what happened. The stench of burned rubber hung in the air. In the intermittent light of passing cars, we saw that both a front and rear tire diagonally opposite each other had blown. We were lucky to be alive, but remained in a dangerous situation stuck on the side of the freeway on a dark night between small, isolated farming communities with two flat tires and only one spare as fast-moving traffic whizzed by mere feet away. Despite the Red Beast's large size, it shuddered each time a car or truck flew by. Being skinny, I caught myself anticipating the sudden gusts and leaning into the wind created by each passing vehicle. At least it was a warm summer night.

A big rig stopped and two men got out. They offered to help. Mom and Mary gratefully accepted. One of the men checked our spare tire. A couple of minutes later, he returned and said to my mother, "The spare's flat too, ma'am."

That surprised me. I could have sworn it looked inflated before we started the trip. Meanwhile, the other man checked the flats, and reported, "Blow-outs. Somebody must have dropped a box of nails."

Mom asked, "Can they be fixed?" Her eyes welled with tears when he explained that the sidewalls were badly damaged and the tires ruined. We were a big family, which meant limited options and even more limited money. Poking her head into the vehicle, Mom reminded the rest of the kids to stay in the car and be still.

"We can take one of you into town, ma'am," one of the truckers offered. "We know a guy who runs a tire shop there. We could call his home and ask him to meet us at his shop. He could help you, maybe sell you a couple new tires."

"Sure, and he'd drive you back here to install them for you," the other trucker added.

Mom said, "That's kind of you. Thank you." She looked at Mary. "I'll go."

Mary looked at the two men and back to my mother, "Are you sure? I don't mind go…"

I didn't want either my mom or Mary to be alone with two strange men on a dark highway, and I knew they didn't want to leave their little ones. As the oldest kid at fifteen—well, almost fifteen and feeling nearly old enough to be a man—I felt it was my responsibility to go. I was a little scared. My stomach churned at the thought, but going with them seemed the best of limited options, all bad.

I wiped my sweaty palms on my jeans and offered, "I'll go, Mom."

My voice cracked. I hoped no one else noticed.

Mom hesitated. She carefully looked at the men, and then glanced at Mary, who replied with a slight shrug, pursed lips, and a "What other choice do we have?" look. The men smiled and seemed friendly enough, so Mom reluctantly agreed to let me go with them. She opened her purse, paused, and looked at the men, "Do you have any idea how much two new tires will cost?"

The taller man replied with a number that made my Mom's eyes grow wide. The man added, "It could be less, but that's what I'd bring just to be sure."

"Don't forget the sales tax," reminded the other man.

Mom began counting out the money. I knew it was coming from the funds our parents had carefully saved all year for this trip. As she added to the pile of bills in my hand, I whispered, "Mom, is there going to be enough left over to go to Disneyland?"

"I don't know, son. We'll have to wait and see." The look in her eyes let me know I was right to worry.

The taller man put the flat spare in a tire rack under their trailer as he said, "We'll also ask our friend to fix or replace your spare. It's never a good idea to drive without a good spare tire."

I saw the worried looks on Mom and Mary's faces as the shorter man opened the passenger-side door of the big rig and said in a friendly voice, "C'mon, young man, climb in."

"Better take your jacket, son. It could get cold," Mom said.

I opened my mouth to argue, but realized it would worsen the embarrassment. My sister held it out a window for me. I grabbed it and grunted a sullen thank-you to her. I waved good-bye to Mom and tried to appear confident as I climbed into the truck's cab.

* * *

The big noisy diesel engine was already running. They'd left it running when they'd gotten out. I'd never been in the cab of a big rig before. I was excited by the opportunity and looked forward to telling my friends about my adventure. I was surprised by how loud the engine was and how much everything shook. The whole cab vibrated. It was dark inside. It felt like I'd climbed into a different world, one that resembled a mysterious, rumbling, cave. At the time, I didn't think to wonder why the truck's dome light didn't come on when the doors opened. The passenger seat must have had an amazing suspension system. It moved when I sat on it, and felt almost as though I was floating on air.

The driver told me to sit in the back. As I turned to do as he said, my right hand touched the top of the driver's seat back. It felt semi-liquid and sticky. I pulled my hand away and wiped it on my jeans. It was too dark to see what it was.

I'd heard that many big rigs had beds behind the front seats so they could sleep at rest stops and not need to stay in motels when on the road. I felt around in the darkness behind the front seats, and sure enough touched what appeared to be a bed. I sat on the edge closest to the front seats and centered so I could see out the front windshield. I didn't want to miss anything.

The engine roared and the cab shuddered as the driver pulled onto the highway. I noticed the extra shifts of gear needed to get up to highway speed. The men didn't say anything.

I stayed on the edge of the bed and hoped the trip to the garage would be short. The novelty quickly wore off. I was tired and becoming bored.

After a few miles, I saw a lighted exit. It beckoned like a glowing oasis shimmering in a desert of darkness. As we drove past, the light lit the truckers' faces for a moment just as the men turned to glance at each other. I'd never seen such cold expressions. Not even in the movies. A chill ran up my spine. Fear grew in me like bamboo in the rainy season. I was afraid to talk to them; but, when I couldn't hold the question within me any longer I finally blurted out, "How much further until we get to the tire shop?"

I hoped I sounded confident and manly, but feared the words just sounded scared and childish. In the near-total darkness I didn't see the burly left arm swing from the passenger seat and back-hand me across my face. The lightning-fast blow flung me across the bed. My head spun. Blood dripped from my split lips.

He growled, "Shut up, kid, and hand me the money your mommy gave you!"

"But…"

"Say another word and I'll kill you."

I reached into my pocket and pulled out the money, and then leaned forward to hand it to him. I said with a sullenness perfected from years of practice as a teenager, "Here."

BLAM! This time his blow knocked me to the back of the sleeping compartment.

"Not. Another. Word."

Both men roared in spirit-crushing laughter at my predicament and weakness.

I lay there, quietly sobbing and keeping my bloody face as far away from his reach as I could. Shame and rage fought for control, and I was the loser. I had to keep my lips pressed tightly together to keep any more of the coppery-salty mixture of blood, tears, and sweat from getting into my mouth. That made my split lips hurt more.

A growing sense of dread consumed the naïve hope that things would turn out fine and I was just over-reacting.

Are they really taking me to the tire shop? If so, why are they being so brutal? What if they aren't *taking me there?* A panic tsunami hit me and left me adrift in a lonely sea of desperation.

Over and over, I mentally replayed what had occurred since I got into the truck, desperate to find clues that might help me to find answers and a way to escape from these men. *What have I missed? What am I missing?* After a couple of minutes, I remembered that my head had hit something harder than the bed. At first, I thought maybe I'd banged it into the wall behind the bed, but whatever I'd hit was softer than a metal wall. I wracked my memory to remember. *My head landed on something that was about eight or nine inches above the bed's surface.*

I leaned backwards, my arms extended behind me, fingers outstretched, and felt behind me in the darkness about where my head had hit. I touched something and it moved! I jerked my hand away. Although slight, that movement petrified me. *Something's alive back here in the dark with me!*

I heard a muffled moan so faint I thought I'd imagined it. Twisting around and feeling my way like a blind man, I realized it was a prone adult. I moved trembling hands in the darkness toward what I hoped was that person's head. My fingertips felt the rise of an Adam's apple and then something scratchy on a chin. *Stubble. A man.*

I reached the area where I thought his mouth would be; but, instead of feeling lips, I touched something flat. The mouth area was covered in the same viscous, sticky substance I'd felt on the top of the driver's seat. My mind raced. Adrenaline surged through me and my body shook. *Blood! It's gotta be blood!* Some kind of wide tape covered his mouth. *Probably duct tape.* Scared almost beyond sanity, I turned to face the front and began to edge further away from whoever shared the bed with me until I remembered the damage the thug-in-the-passenger-seat's arm inflicted. I decided the unknown man was safer than creeps up front and edged backward an inch or two. I felt as though I balanced on the edge of a razor blade. It was painful to stay where I was, but it would be worse if I moved.

At least the man's still alive. That's something. He's gagged, but is he tied up? He must be; but, if he's not, maybe we can work together to get out of here. I leaned back and groped for his hands. I touched a place of ridges and gaps. It took me a second to figure it out. *Fingers!* I moved my fingers in the gaps between his fingers to the back of one of his hands and onto something smooth wrapped around his wrists. *Damn! Duct tape!*

I turned back around and belatedly noticed that even the instrument lights on the rig's dashboard had been turned way down low. *No wonder it's so dark in here.* I tried to learn as much as I could about the men and memorize their faces in those precious moments when we passed under lit signs and occasional highway lights on all-too-infrequent overpasses. They had been careful not to address each other by name, so I made up my own. In the flash of an overpass light, I caught a glimpse of the driver as he took a large swig from a whiskey bottle. *Boozer.* The one on the passenger side had a surprisingly round nose and wild, frizzy hair. He reminded me of a toy clown I'd had as a young kid. Bozo. He was my favorite toy, with a painted plastic head and stuffed cloth body. I'd accidentally left it in our front yard one evening. The next morning my beloved friend had been torn to shreds and scattered all over our yard, presumably by the neighbor's dog which was known to run loose. I don't think I ever wanted another plush toy after losing Bozo. *I wish some big dog would tear this Bozo and his boozing buddy apart. I wouldn't mourn their loss for a second!*

At that moment, Bozo said in a tone that sounded more like a whine than a request, "Let me have some of that."

"No! I already gave you some. I bought it. The rest is mine." The snarl left no room for doubt that Bozo wasn't getting any more of Boozer's whiskey.

Okay. Boozer's the boss. Good to know. Just gotta stay away from Bozo's arm.

A few minutes later, Bozo said, "Gotta put on the other license plates and reconnect the lights on the trailer. Don't wanna get stopped."

Boozer grunted. "Whadja do with the license plates you took off that broken-down truck?"

"Got 'em right here."

Several miles later, Boozer took an off-ramp and pulled to the side of an unlit, two-lane road. He shut off the headlights but kept the engine running. A flood of darkness engulfed me, so oppressive I felt I might suffocate.

Boozer turned to Bozo and, as he opened the door to get out, snarled, "Watch the scrawny runt. Try not to kill him. He's worth more alive."

As Boozer stepped down, I saw the door of my cage was open. Animal instinct, panic, and adrenaline instantly boiled over into a toxic cocktail of temporary insanity. I didn't think, just bolted for the opening. Bad idea! The front seats were configured in such a way that I couldn't just lunge for the open door. I had to try to burst through the space between the seats in the middle of the cab, get past Bozo, then twist ninety degrees, squeeze past the steering wheel, and lunge face-first out the cab maybe five feet onto the pavement below, still evading Boozer's grasp.

Bozo must have anticipated my move. It was practically over before it began. I got as far as thrusting my head between the seats. THWUMP!

* * *

Darkness, disorientation, and pain. *Where am I? Why does my head throb?* I shook the cobwebs out of my brain, but that made my head hurt even more. My skull felt split wide open. Blood dripped down the side of my head, around the front of my right ear, and traced my jaw as it trickled down my neck.

I lay on my right side, facing the back of the cab. I tried to sit up, but discovered that my arms and legs were bound at the wrists and ankles. Sitting took extraordinary effort, a combination of rolling, jabbing elbows, and the exercise of abdominal muscles that I wished were stronger.

I probed my head wound and my mouth. *I know that smell. Duct Tape.* I tried to find the edge of the tape so I could pinch it with my fingers or scratch it of with my fingernails and pull it off. I felt around the right side of my mouth and followed the tape all the way to the back of my neck. With a sinking feeling— and already knowing what I'd find—I repeated the process from the left side of my mouth. I then wasted several minutes, trying to feel a slight ridge on the smooth tape where I might still be able to find an end.

Damn! Nothing! I roared inwardly. *They wrapped it around my whole head and left no loose ends to pull off!*

A long exhale through my nose summed up my frustration as I lowered my bound hands to my lap. All I'd managed to do with my stupid, impulsive move was to make my situation far worse. *Great! Now I'm hurt and tied up. Way to go, genius! Well, at least my blood's making a mess all over their truck!* I thought spitefully. *That'll teach 'em!*

But I knew I was the one who'd been taught a lesson. I hoped I'd learned it well enough to keep from getting hit again. I didn't know how much blood I'd lost, but knew I only had a limited supply and wanted to keep as much of it as I could. Stinging sweat dripped into my eyes. I closed and rubbed them, replacing near-total darkness with bottom-of-a-mile-deep pit utter darkness. The kind that reminded me I was utterly alone.

A few minutes later, morbid humor came to me: *Well, at least I haven't peed my pants yet.* I made yet another mistake. The thought of peeing reminded my bladder that it was full and would need to be emptied sooner rather than later. *Damn it!*

As if on cue, the smell of urine filled the air. *No way! That can't be me, can it?* Hands still in my lap, I touched my crotch. *Dry! Thank God! Must be that man back here. I hope Boozer and Bozo don't smell it. It might piss them off.* I realized the inadvertent pun. In any other situation, I would have laughed at my cleverness. Now, I just hung my aching, bloody head, chin on my chest and cried.

The pity party lasted a while longer, then I raised my head and tried to look around. It was still dark. The dim, eerie glow of the dashboard displays offered the only light. We were moving again. The bumpier road sounds and lack of lights of oncoming cars informed me that we weren't on the freeway anymore.

They must have turned off the freeway while I was knocked out. Where are we? Where are they taking me? They don't seem to want to kill me. At least not yet. But why did they take me? And who is on the bed behind me? Is he still alive?

I slowly turned around in the dark, careful not to make a sound. I guessed at where I thought the man's head might be and extended my hands, hoping I'd be able to feel his breath on them. I got the correct location, but misjudged the distance in the darkness and bumped him in what felt like his nose. He flinched and softly moaned. I yanked my hands away.

Sorry. I'm glad you're alive, I thought to him, not daring to make a sound for fear of being hit again.

I thought of Mom, Mary, and all the kids stuck on the side of a dark freeway in the middle of nowhere counting on us— counting on *me*—to help them. Tears resumed falling and I sobbed, quietly, gasping for air through my nose. *I'm sorry, Mom. Can't help you. Haven't even been able to help myself. I hope you're all safe.* Weeping clogged my sinuses and made my nose run, making it harder to breathe. Panicking, I tried sniffling, but snot leaked back down again, so I pushed my nose into the notch where my chest joined my left arm and blew. That seemed to help, so I blew again as forcefully and quietly as I could until my nose was mostly clear. *That was a close call. Okay. No more crying. Time to man up, you big baby, before you suffocate.*

Another thought came to me, one a golden ray of hope piercing the darkness. *Maybe the highway patrol found everyone and got them to safety. At least you'll all be safe. Have I been gone long enough for you to worry about me yet? How long was I knocked out? It's still dark outside. Couldn't have been too long.*

We rolled on, mile after mile, the darkness pierced only by the rig's headlights and occasionally the lights of an oncoming vehicle or a lonely house standing sentinel among dark fields. I craved light of any kind and was grateful for even the briefest moment when any light came into view. Light gave me hope. *Will this night ever end? If it does, will I still be alive to see it?*

Bozo turned to Boozer, and asked, "When we stopped to change the truck's plates, did you remember to ditch the Travelall's spare tire?"

Boozer ignored him and took a long gulp of whiskey.

"I asked, when you…"

Boozer growled, "I heard you the first time! Quit worrying! It's gone. Rolled it far enough from the road it won't be found. What did you find in the kid's pockets?"

"Damn little: A cheap wallet with $17 and a photo of a young girl, a comb, and a handkerchief. Not even a pocketknife."

Bozo thought for a moment, and then asked, "Any chance we'll get caught?"

"For the third time: No!" Boozer added, "Those two broads were so shaken up by their spin-out they won't be able to ID us or the truck. It was dark. Our hats were pulled down over our eyes. Any traffic going by would have backlit us. Besides, this truck was headed for Mexico City. Won't be missed for days. We'll reach our buyer in Tijuana in a few hours. Gonna be the easiest money we ever made."

Those words darkened any glimmers of hope.

"Those poor bastards in Mexico City!" Bozo chuckled.

"Yeah. Poor bastards. News said it was a huge quake. Who knows? Maybe our buyer will sell this load of medical supplies back to 'em on the black market," he added with a cruel laugh.

Bozo joined in. "Yeah, wouldn't that be something? And your idea to take the trucker and the boy was pure genius."

"Buyer said some folks were desperate for fresh body parts," Boozer replied.

"Can't get any fresher than the ones inside that kid, but I'd hoped one of the broads would have come with us instead. We could have had fun before selling her for parts," Bozo chortled.

I flinched and suddenly felt a fresh wave of panic and nausea roll over me. Burning bile rose in my throat. But, with my taped mouth, there was there was nowhere for it to go but back down again. *My God! I've got to get out of here! At least Mom and Mary are safe from these monsters.* Pride mixed in with the panic and nausea bubbling within me. *I won't have died for nothing. Stop thinking like that!*

Boozer took another swig of whiskey and belched. The reek added to my nausea. "The old guy still alive?"

"I checked after tying up the kid. The geezer was still alive then. Barely, but he was still breathing."

"Offering to give me a ride is the last mistake he'll ever make," Boozer said with a malevolent chuckle.

"I wish you hadn't hit him so hard."

"The empty bottle was handy. Besides, I was the one who sat on the piece of broken glass. My ass still hurts."

Bozo complained, "He might die before we get to our buyer."

"We'll soon be there. His organs could still be fresh enough. Either way, we're gonna be *rich* when we sell the truck, all the medical supplies, and the kid's body parts!"

My mind raced. I tried to ignore the "kid's body parts" comment. *Did I hear them say "broken glass?" That sticky liquid I felt on the top of the driver's seat must have been blood. Boozer must have smashed a bottle over the driver's head as the old guy sat in the driver's seat. The bottle must have shattered. Maybe some shards fell on the floor back here or in the space between the seats in the front.*

I lowered my taped hands and brushed the tips of my fingers along the floor. I felt around in the dark, inch by inch, hoping my movements wouldn't be visible, especially if lit up by the sudden lights of an eighteen-wheeler heading around a corner from the other direction.

A stabbing pain in my middle finger rewarded my careful search. I grunted from the shock and froze, afraid I'd been heard; but the drone of the engine and road noise must have drowned out the sound. I gingerly felt around a shard that appeared to be about an inch wide and two-and-a-half inches long. One end was rounded and smooth. It must have been part of the mouth of the bottle. The other end was sharp and pointed. *Perfect!*

I attempted to grasp it with the fingers of my right hand. It kept sliding along the floor or slipping from my fingers and falling. I tried again and again, fearful the shard would fall where I wouldn't be able to reach it, or I'd be caught and beaten again, or worse. The pointed end stuck me twice and one of the sharp edges cut the tip of my index finger. After the first shock, I was prepared for the pain and didn't make a sound. Unfortunately, the blood smearing the glass made my task even harder.

I managed to pinch the smooth, curved end between my thumb and first two fingers. I tried to bend and twist my hands towards my wrists in every way I could think of. No matter what I did, I couldn't touch the shard to the duct tape. I started to reach up to try to put the shard between my teeth but remembered the duct tape over my mouth. I considered bringing my knees up to my chest to try to cut the tape holding my legs together at the ankles, but feared such contortions would alert Bozo. I didn't want to risk losing the shard I'd worked so hard to find, not to mention the beating he'd give me or worse. Every muscle in my body tensed from frustration.

* * *

"I think I see a cop." My head jerked up. Bozo must have been looking at his side view mirror.

"Where?"

"Behind us."

Boozer looked out his side mirror, stared for a moment, and said, "Yeah." He looked at the speedometer. "I'm not speeding. We should be okay."

They continued to look at their mirrors.

I hoped to have time to cut myself free before making my move, but having a cop so close might be my best chance. Maybe my only chance. *No time to think. Now or never!* I leaned forward, just in front of the driver's seat headrest, and jammed the point of the shard as deeply into Boozer's neck as I could and began to pull it toward me to create as much damage as possible. He yelped and jerked his neck away while using his right hand to try to bat away whatever was hurting him. The truck swerved as he fought to control the bleeding and the metal monster. The shard slipped from my blood-soaked fingers and I fell backward.

Bozo jerked away from the side mirror and screamed, *"What?"*

"The kid just cut me! Gimme your handkerchief! I'm bleeding like a stuck pig."

Bozo fumbled with his seat belt latch, undid it, steadied himself with his left hand as he retrieved his handkerchief from his right rear pants pocket, and shoved it into the wound.

"Oww! Be careful, you idiot!," he screamed. "Get the kid! Be careful. I don't know what he cut me with!"

After falling, I couldn't regain my balance to sit up as the truck swerved out of control. Every time I'd almost gotten into a sitting position, the swaying cab would tip me over again.

Boozer fought to stop the blood flowing from his neck with his right hand while trying to regain control of the wildly swerving rig with his left.

In the side mirrors I saw the lights on top of the police cruiser light up as its siren's blare filled the air.

Bozo turned to face me. I didn't have to see his eyes to see my death.

I remembered my jacket and grabbed it in an attempt to fling it into his face. However, I must have been lying on an arm of it because it felt like it pivoted and, for a moment, froze in mid-air in front of him. The sudden appearance of something touching his nose and outside edges of his face in must have startled Bozo. He reacted the way someone does who hates spiders and has just walked face-first into a large web: he flailed his arms to remove whatever had touched his face in the dark.

I fell back and kicked Bozo in the face with my bound feet. It was a hard, but glancing, blow.

Bozo's head jerked back, and he clutched whatever he could to regain his balance, grabbing along Boozer's right arm and then the steering wheel as he fell, jerking the steering wheel and the rig sharply to the right. Boozer panicked and locked the brakes. Bozo's body weight and the truck's momentum worked against him. He flew head first into the windshield as the truck ran into a big irrigation ditch. When his head hit, the glass cracked, but held. Seconds later, it shattered and gave way as the truck smashed into the ditch's far bank. The rig's headlights illuminating the ditch revealed that Bozo's head was no longer inside the truck's cab.

I crashed against the back of the passenger seat. The captive trucker's body slammed into me as I bounced back. Fortunately for both of us, the tops of our heads faced in opposite directions. As it was, our faces both got a painful acquaintance with each other's feet. From the wheezing sound Boozer made when his torso slammed into the steering wheel, he might have busted some ribs.

The big rig tilted toward its right side. Boozer roared, "I'll break your neck, you little r—!"

The passenger side door flew open. A police officer stuck her head and flashlight into the cab and yelled, "Are you oka—"

She jerked backward at the sight of Bozo's headless torso sliding toward her. She fell against the bank. Boozer tried to open his door, but the heavy panel was at just enough of an angle to make it difficult to open upward. With his back to me, I thrust my bound hands through the opening in the seats hoping the officer could see them. Boozer let the driver-side door fall back into place and then tried to rush through the passenger door, crawl-falling as he climbed over Bozo's carcass.

I lunged for his feet; afraid he might overpower the stunned officer as he fell onto her. If she hadn't seen my taped hands she'd have no way of knowing the situation was anything other than an accident until it was too late. I tried grunting to warn her, but doubted she could hear me over the noise of the engine. I was able to grab one of Boozer's ankles, but gravity and Boozer's body weight prevented me from doing anything more than slow him down for a moment, despite my pushing off the side of the passenger seat using my feet for leverage.

Boozer used his free foot to kick the other one free and stretched out his hands to keep from landing face-first onto the side of the bank. The patrolwoman must have caught a glimpse of the bloody duct tape on my wrists, because she rolled to the side just out of his reach. He turned his head to the right just in time for the muzzle of the officer's handgun to jam into his nose.

She yelled into the cab, "Hang on! You're safe. One of us will be with you in a minute." She cuffed Boozer and began walking him to her patrol car. The medical units and backup she summoned on her radio soon arrived. I looked over at the old trucker, and saw him move in the kaleidoscopic flashing lights. *Help's coming. We're gonna make it, old-timer. Hang in there.*

With my feet still jammed against the inside edge of the passenger seat, I looked out the front windshield and saw dawn's first light pierce the darkness. I stretched upward, inching my way to the outside edge of the driver's side seat between it and the door and pulled the air horn cord to announce to the world that our desperate journey was over. Somehow, I'd made it to the light of dawn after the longest and darkest night of my life. I collapsed from exhaustion, still pulling that cord until a patrolman gently pried it from my trembling, bloody hands.

No Choice at All

Daniel Hansen was angry, something he rarely felt for long. He glared at the flat tire delaying him from getting to the most important meeting of his career. It didn't help that it was a dark winter night, the car was a rental, the model unfamiliar to him, and the tire iron and jack were in separate hidden compartments, one of which was under the bolted-down spare. What should have been a ten- or fifteen-minute job took him an agonizingly long thirty-five minutes.

With the spare finally in place and tightened down, Daniel threw the flat in the trunk and slammed the lid. He took a step in the direction of the driver's door. Thunk. *What the hell?* He bent down to see what he'd stepped on. The tire iron was still lying in the dirt where he'd accidentally left it in his haste to get back on the road. *Damn!* Frustration welled up within him. For a moment as it laid there he considered tossing it into the bushes. *Calm down! That's not going to help anything!* Daniel shook his head in disgust, grabbed the annoying metal bar, got behind the wheel, and slammed the tire iron on the seat beside him. He started the car and floored it back onto the road.

Damn! So much for having extra time. Might still be okay if I don't have any more delays. I may even have time to wash my hands. I had no idea The Dragon lived so far out in the sticks! Even this winding road is slowing me down! At least there's no traffic! Haven't seen anyone for nearly half an hour. Hate to get behind a slow driver. That's all I'd need!

His headlights tore into the darkness. Daniel increased his speed as much as he dared. He was a good driver, but this curving two-lane road would be unforgiving if he became careless. He'd learned a thing or two in his thirty-two years. *No sense taking crazy chances.* But every mile gained cost him precious minutes. His mind raced faster than his car traveled. *Maybe I should call to say I might be late. No, that would just make me later, and there's still a chance I'll make it on time. Besides, tucked in between these mountains I doubt if my phone would even have a signal.*

He willed himself to calm down and just focus on the road. Instead of fighting the asphalt curves, he used them as he got back into a rhythm with the road.

It was a surprisingly warm evening this high up in the mountains. Daniel drove with his windows open, enjoying the fresh air.

His headlights briefly swept over two cars parked on the opposite side of the road as he rounded a curve and picked up speed. He caught a glimpse of them as he drove by. The dome light of the front car was on as he approached but went out as he was nearly abreast of it. Daniel continued on his way.

That's odd. The light went out, but the car's doors were open. Well, there could be good reasons for that.

Daniel thought back to the scene as he drove, and decided other things didn't seem quite right. Some men were on each side of the car. They'd frozen as he drove past.

A woman in a car with at least three men standing around it. Why would the men freeze like that when I drove by? Strange. On a dark road. In the middle of nowhere. Maybe they're just kids having fun. No. The driver looked old enough to be their mother, and the men looked more like adults than teens. Don't overreact. It may be nothing. Something innocent. Maybe they're helping her fix her car. And don't forget your interview. Stop now, and you can kiss that promotion and maybe even your career at the company goodbye. What a choice!

Except, he knew it was no choice at all.

* * *

Daniel Hansen's boss, Harrison "The Dragon" Dunsmuir, was a stickler for punctuality and many other things. No one ever called him "The Dragon" to his face, of course, but several people swore they actually saw fire spew from his mouth when he was angry. Daniel had seen a bit of Dunsmuir's temper, but, thankfully, it had always been directed at someone else. In every case, the young executive felt The Dragon was tough but fair.

Daniel began working for Dunsmuir Technologies right out of college. Its many advances in critical life-saving medical technologies had attracted him. Having lost a mother to cancer while still in his mid-teens, he wanted to do his part in helping others escape such pain. Daniel rapidly rose through the ranks and turned a poorly performing division into a well-oiled machine. His employees loved his collaborative leadership style, how he acknowledged and publicly praised individual and team efforts, exhibited confidence without arrogance, and set tough but achievable goals.

His rugged good looks, and thick, unruly hair, turning salt-and-pepper at the sideburns of his clean-shaven face, attracted women. He wasn't particularly athletic, but he swam almost daily. Although Daniel was not quite six feet tall, people—even those who were taller than he—looked up to him. Some of his female coworkers tried flirting with him. He politely and gracefully fended off the more ardent advances. Completely focused on his job, Daniel never dated anyone from the company.

Of thirty-seven major operating groups company-wide, his unit's results had improved under his leadership from the second-worst in the company to being within a hair's breadth of the company's best division. His unit gained ground on the coveted number one spot every month. Although located far from company headquarters, his group and their successes had quickly come to Dunsmuir's attention.

When the top executive of the division that was the company's crowning jewel announced his retirement, Daniel received the opportunity to interview for the position to replace him. He'd felt doubly honored to receive the invitation to meet at Dunsmuir's home in the country. No one at his level had ever been invited to what the employees secretly called The Dragon's Lair. He had tough competition for this job from both inside and outside the company. Showing up late and with dirty hands could ruin his chances for this job, and perhaps any other opportunities with the firm. Executives at his level were supposed to anticipate and head off problems before they occurred, and to build in sufficient extra time to cover any contingencies. Daniel was especially proud that he'd never missed a deadline at work. Tardiness was simply not an option, but late arrival at a meeting with the Dragon in his Lair was unthinkable.

Daniel found a place to turn around. *How many curves has the road made since I saw the cars? Two? No, three, and the last one was long and gradual. You better be right.* He drove past two curves, shut off his headlights, and quietly eased off the road before the third. He parked and shut off his dome light. *No sense warning them I'm coming.* Daniel estimated he was about an eighth of a mile away from the people in the clearing. As he opened his door, he heard a woman scream. It was faint from the distance but unmistakable. He pulled his out his phone and tried to dial 911. *Damn! No signal!*

Daniel had never been a violent man. Other than a couple of minor skirmishes in high school when he'd stood up for people being bullied, he'd never been in a fight in his life. He had no idea how he'd do if it came to a fight tonight. *There are at least three men. What if they have weapons? What the hell are you doing, Daniel? You're a business executive, not Superman!*

From the corner of his eye in the dim glow from his phone, he saw the tire iron. A terrifying thought came to him. *What if they have guns?* That triggered the memory of an old joke: "Never take a knife to a gunfight." *It's no doubt true for tire irons, too.* He reached over and grabbed it anyway. A bent piece of metal was better than no weapon at all.

As Daniel got out of his car and carefully eased the door closed, he heard another distant scream. This one sounded like it may have come from a man. *Gotta hurry!*

He ran along the side of the road most of the way, and then carefully pushed into the edge of the woods to conceal himself among the trees and brush as he got to within fifty yards of the clearing. Daniel cautiously placed his feet to make the least possible noise and to avoid tripping. Despite his efforts, he had no choice but to step on dry leaves and small twigs. Every sound was magnified a thousand times by his adrenaline-charged imagination. *Jeez, Daniel. A blindfolded, drunk elephant would make less noise!*

He slowed further as he neared the clearing and ducked behind a tree a dozen feet in front of the grill of what he figured was the woman's car. Daniel wiped sweat off his forehead with the back of his hand to keep it from dripping into his eyes. He quickly tried to orient himself and figure out what was going on. Daniel leaned forward and squinted as his eyes worked to make the most of the pale glow of a crescent moon that was partially obscured by large patches of slowly drifting clouds.

He focused on a man and slender, blonde woman who stood facing each other a few yards across from the open passenger side door. Another man crept up behind her.

There must be at least two women. This one's much younger than the one I saw earlier. Looks about twenty-eight or thirty.

Without warning the man facing the younger woman backhanded her with a savage blow. Her whole body spun in the direction her head had been whipped. She lost her balance and fell onto her back.

"That's more like it! Let's do her here," said the man on the other side of her. The woman struck out with her arms and legs, but the men stayed just out of range of her kicks and blows.

"No. Someone might see or hear us here. We already had a close call with that car awhile ago," the man who hit her replied.

The woman tried to get up, but he grabbed her by the hair and threw her back down. "Not so fast!"

He nodded toward what appeared to be a trail head. "Let's take her down there."

The man near the woman's feet grumbled at the delay, and tried to grab her flailing feet while the other tried to do the same with her wrists. After several tries, they captured her ankles and wrists, one in each hand. They lifted and carried her toward the trail.

She thrashed like a wounded lioness. They'd only gone about ten feet when her wild contortions made the man at her legs lose his grip on one of her ankles. His hand slipped onto one of her shoes. She pulled her foot free. The shoe went flying as he lunged to re-capture her foot. She grunted and kicked with all her might, smashing the sole of her bare foot into the man's left kneecap. He bellowed and grabbed his knee, slamming the bent leg straight.

"Damn it, Jake! Hold her still while I grab her again," the wounded man yelled.

Jake's laugh was vicious. "That'll teach you for letting go. Grab her and hang on this time!"

The man with the sore kneecap recaptured her loose leg, and they headed for the trees with their thrashing cargo, going a little slower due to the trailing man's limp.

Daniel turned his attention to the older woman in the car. She still sat behind the steering wheel, hands grasping the top of it, and occasionally letting go of it with her left hand to punch at the man standing in the open driver's doorway. He easily avoided her blows and then grabbed her hair as she gasped and jerked her head away. Another man kept reaching through the open front passenger door and appeared to be playfully grabbing for and slapping at her legs. They reminded him of cats toying with a wounded mouse before killing it. Those two men seemed to at least initially be more interested in terrorizing her than doing physical harm to her, and she appeared to be using her position inside the car to keep them at bay.

Two more men. Shit. Four.

Daniel couldn't think of a way to take on all four men at once. The two men carrying the woman down the trail were helping him by moving away from the others. *If I get really lucky, I might only have to only face two-to-one odds twice instead of four-to-one all at once. Who am I kidding? Those odds still suck! I'd never bet my life on those odds.* But he knew that's exactly what he was doing. *If, by some miracle, I get lucky with the first two, I'll have the "opportunity" to risk my life again with the other two. Quit whining! You've got work to do.*

The woman being carried down the trail appeared to be in the most immediate danger. He couldn't walk into the clearing to follow the ones on the trail without a high probability of being seen. If he were too close to the trail, the men carrying the blonde would probably hear him before he could reach them. Even with "only" two against one, Daniel knew he needed the element of surprise. He decided to make a wide arc around them. *I should be able travel faster than two men carrying a thrashing woman, especially with one of them limping. Might be able to cut 'em off and surprise 'em.*

No part of the plan worked as he'd hoped. It was slow going over and around fallen trees and large bushes. Then Daniel ran into a large thicket with spiky thorns. He tried to find a way around the barbed beast, but ultimately gave up and powered his way through it, getting scratched, stuck, and gouged every painful step of the way. He finally reached the last of the thicket only to face an outcropping that cut off his intended route and forced him into a ravine that sent him two hundred feet in the wrong direction until he found a way to climb out of it. *Way to go, Superman! I'm tired, scratched, gasping for air, bleeding, and my suit is shredded—and I haven't even had to try to take on the four men yet!*

The two men dragged the younger woman deep into the woods, so no one from the road would be able to hear them. She screamed and struggled the whole way. They didn't want to take any more chances.

Kneecap shouted, "Hellcat! The more you fight, the more fun we'll have, and the longer it's going to last."

They found a clearing just big enough for what they had in mind and dropped her in the middle of it. Landing on her back knocked the wind out of her. The desperate woman changed tactics, stalling for time to catch her breath. She rolled onto her left side, curled into a fetal position, pulled her knees tightly to her chest, and bear-hugged her lower legs.

The men laughed at her antics. Leaning forward to pull her arms from around her legs, they bumped heads. Their laughter stopped. The woman used the opportunity to release her legs and kick at Kneecap's sore knee. Wise to her moves, he sidestepped the attack, then flopped diagonally across her outstretched legs with his torso centered over her knees, pinning her right knee on top of her left.

She pounded Kneecap's head with her fists. Jake laughed at the beating his friend was taking as he grabbed her flailing wrists. He got down onto his hands and knees, his body extended away from her prone head, his nose near enough to her face to smell her perfume. Jake used his superior body weight to hold her slender wrists in position and smirked at her. "Time for a kiss, Hellcat."

She smelled cheap booze and body odor as he as he leaned toward her. She jerked her head upward and smashed her forehead into his mouth and the lower part of nose. Jake screamed and jerked his head away, barely able to keep holding onto her wrists.

It was Kneecap's turn to laugh as he saw his accomplice's bloody mouth and nose. "Not so funny now, huh, Jake?"

Kneecap tore at Hellcat's clothes as his fellow attacker tried to slow the bleeding by pressing his nose and lips against the upper arm of his shirtsleeve while still holding her down.

She was fierce and tenacious, but they were bigger. Stronger. Heavier. And, there were two of them. She was losing the battle. It was only a matter of time.

The older woman's situation worsened by the moment. The man near the open drivers side door looked over the roof of her car and yelled to his accomplice, "Enough games! Let's drag her out and do her."

She moved the moment her attackers took their eyes off her to look at each other. She'd been waiting for just such an opportunity. She turned the key in the ignition and the engine roared to life. The startled men instinctively leaned toward her just as she threw the car into Drive and hit the gas. The car leapt forward with a roar and knocked both men to the ground. The woman turned on her headlights and aimed the car in the direction she'd seen the other men go as they dragged her daughter away.

The trail was only wide enough for people to walk in single-file. Thick brush, saplings, and occasionally bigger trees, grew close on both sides of it. The car straddled the trail as she furiously yanked the steering wheel back and forth to dodge bigger trees and gullies, frantic to get to her daughter as her car cut crashed through and rolled over bushes and saplings. Gravity and the car's big engine were her allies as the vehicle surged against the bushes and trees that worked to stop her. The men who had assaulted her quickly gained ground, cursing as they pursued her.

* * *

Daniel crept into position about eight feet behind the man called Jake. Being so outnumbered, Daniel knew that, if he knocked any of them down, then he needed to make sure they *stayed* down. He lunged toward Jake just as they all heard what sounded like a banshee far up the trail. Jake got off his hands, rose to his knees, and turned toward the noise when his attacker smashed the tire iron into the base of his skull. Daniel heard the sickening crunch and felt it vibrate up the bar into his arms. Kneecap jerked his head up and saw Jake crumple like a rag doll.

He leapt to his feet, pushing his long, lank hair away from his eyes. Daniel sprang toward him, slashing with the tire iron, hoping to hit the thug in the throat before he could shout a warning to the others. His eyes were focused on Kneecap, and he tripped on the thrashing woman's head. Instead of delivering a crushing blow, the tire iron only clawed the air as Kneecap jerked backwards. Daniel turned his head just in time to avoid having his nose smack into the dirt as he crashed lengthwise on top of the flailing blonde, his face colliding with the desperate woman's feet as his fist holding the tire iron hit the ground next to them. Despite the impact, he managed to keep his grip on it. Kneecap sidestepped to the right and pounced on him cross-ways, so he could pin down both opponents while keeping his hands free to disarm the lone hand that held the tire iron.

Being trapped on his belly between the writhing woman and his attacker put Daniel at a major disadvantage. His left hand was stuck in a nearly useless position with minimal range of motion as he ineffectively struck at Kneecap's side. The would-be rapist used both his hands to pry Daniel's fingers off the one thing that gave him any chance at all against his three remaining opponents.

Legs and torso pinned by the crushing weight of the two struggling men, Hellcat could only draw shallow breaths. Terror, lack of air, and flagging strength pulled at her consciousness. But her head and arms were free. Desperate, she snagged Kneecap's leg with her left arm and bit into his calf as hard as she could, holding on like a pit bull. Her victim bellowed and tried to yank his leg away.

The sudden, excruciating pain in his leg drove Kneecap to release his right hand from Daniel's fist and reach around to punch Hellcat in the head to make her let go—the move she'd hoped for. She grabbed a handful of dirt with her right hand and ground it into his open-mouthed face as he bellowed, then followed through by clawing his cheek.

Temporarily blinded and with a nose and mouth full of dirt, Kneecap could neither yell nor fight. He needed to inhale after expelling so much air from his bellow; but, when he did, he sucked some of the dirt from his nose and mouth into his air passages and down his throat. He coughed and spluttered. Enraged, he let go of Daniel's hand still clenched around the tire iron, as his only thought became to kill the woman who tormented him.

Daniel seized the opportunity to twist his body at the waist and swing the tire iron up and backwards toward the back of Kneecap's head. His awkward position delivered only a glancing blow to the back of Kneecap's head. But it was enough. The thug collapsed onto the woman's right side and didn't move.

Hellcat writhed, still pinned under both men. She looked in the direction of the clearing and yelled, "The other men have Mom!"

Daniel heaved, dislodging Kneecap, and crawled off the young woman. Both winded and woozy, they hung onto each other to get to their feet, and then stumbled up the path toward her mother.

They heard a loud bang followed by what sounded like metal scraping along rock, close and on or near the trail above them. They rounded a tight bend, Hellcat in front, limping on one bare foot. Ahead and off to her right, she saw her mother's car turned halfway on its passenger side at the bottom of a shallow gully. Her mother's pursuers reached the car first and climbed down the gully to get to the drivers side door. Both panted from the unexpected and infuriating chase.

One bent over, resting one hand on his knee, as he caught his breath. The other at the car's driver's side rear quarter panel gasped, "Let's leave her. She's not worth it!"

The other growled, "She's seen our faces! We agreed no witnesses! Remember?"

It was as though they'd waved a red flag at a bull. Hellcat's nostrils flared. Daniel caught her just in time to keep her from running at the men with her fists flying. She opened her mouth to protest, but he clamped a hand over her mouth. She bit him.

"Ouch!" He urgently whispered, as he pulled her back out of sight behind the sharp curve in the trail, "Stop that! Be still and listen to me."

He hung on tightly to the struggling woman. Her furious eyes burned holes in his soul. She finally stopped writhing, turned to look up into his eyes, and nodded. Daniel returned her nod and cautiously let go of her as he removed his hand from her mouth.

"We're more likely to save your mother if we work together and make a plan."

"You're right. Sorry." She heaved a shuddering breath. She whispered loudly as the thoughts came to her, "She might be hurt from the crash. Maybe she can't defend herself. I didn't see her."

They peeked around the curve in the trail. As if on cue, the older women opened the front passenger side door. Blood dripped down her arm onto her fingers. Facing downhill, the door opened with greater force than she'd intended. The car teetered, swaying further, closer to landing on its side. She lost her grip on the armrest and slid into the door. It fell several inches into the dirt and got wedged open. The older woman's bloody hand reached through the narrow opening and touched the soil.

She seemed so close escaping.

Her captors leaned over to look down through the closed drivers side window to see how the old woman had fared in the crash. They laughed. Her arm stuck out the opening, her neck bent at a painful angle, and her shoulder pressed against the partially-open front passenger door. A large cut near her hairline dripped blood. The woman's feet were uphill, pointing toward the driver's side door.

She struggled to find something to grab to pull herself around and get her head above her feet. She was fighting gravity and losing. The blood made everything slippery.

One of the men taunted, "Come out, come out, wherever you are."

Daniel recognized him as the one who had pulled her hair in the clearing.

A defiant voice replied from inside the car, "Go to hell! If you big, bad, boys want me, you're going to have to come in and get me!"

Hair-puller's sidekick screamed, "That's it! I'm going in after her!" He reached for the handle of the drivers side door.

Hair-puller grabbed his arm and pulled it back. "I've got a better idea. C'mon help me."

He pushed against the side of the car and began rocking it.

"Yeah!" Sidekick laughed. "I like your idea even better! Let's see how many times we can make it roll!"

He leaned toward the car to help push it.

Daniel and Hellcat heard every word as they sneaked back up the trail to a point above where the car had bounced off a tree and down into the gully. They moved slowly and quietly, using the near-darkness of the night and height of the trail to keep out of sight. They crept into position atop the left bank, a few feet above and behind the two men.

The wide arc made by the rocking car forced the men to adjust their centers of gravity to keep from falling with it once the vehicle began to roll. Hellcat screamed and jumped onto Hair-puller's back as he repositioned himself for another push. The unexpected weight forced his hands to slip off the car and over his head as his face smashed into the metal body. Hair-puller and Hellcat slid down into the tight space between the left bank of the gully and drivers side of the rocking car. Hair-puller rolled to his back on top of her as she tried to reach around and gouge his face. He tried to head-butt her, but she dodged the blow.

Sidekick turned to see what happened to his buddy. His feet slipped on the side of the bank and just when Daniel pounced, swinging the tire iron. Sidekick saw it just in time to try to deflect it with his left arm. The curved iron bar shattered his wrist. He screamed and ducked. Momentum carried Daniel over his target and he crashed into the side of the teetering car. Sidekick found his footing, pushed up, his body uncoiling like a spring. He hit Daniel in the gut. Daniel dropped the tire iron as he doubled over, both hands clutching his stomach.

Faint moonlight gleamed on the steel. Sidekick and Daniel dove for the weapon as it bounced against the bank and slid toward the narrow space between the car and the dirt. Both men grabbed hold of the iron bar and tugged on it. Daniel's two good hands gave him an advantage as they leaned on the now nearly motionless car, but Sidekick kicked him in the shin. Daniel grunted and squatted at an angle on the bank, while using his left arm to balance himself on the car. He was ready when Sidekick tried to kick him again, this time in the face.

Daniel ducked under the off-balanced kick. He sprang upward, grabbed the underside of Sidekick's extended leg, and shoved. With his leg jerked skyward, Sidekick's other foot shot out from under him. He landed on his back, head facing uphill, stunned.

Daniel walked up to him and said, "You like kicks so much, huh? How about these?"

He kicked him in the groin. "That's for the women."

Sidekick's scream lasted less than a second, as Daniel's ruined wingtip shoe connected with his face. "That's for me."

Sidekick went limp.

A yelp and sharp exhale following the thud of impact caught Daniel's attention. He glanced back to see Hellcat doubled-over from a punch to the stomach. Daniel took a big breath as he turned to face the fourth assailant. *Three down, one to…* Hair-puller had left Hellcat wheezing on the ground so he could tackle Daniel. Knocking Daniel to the ground, he straddled the fallen man and pummeled him. Daniel tried to block the blows, but too many landed too hard.

Crunch!

Hair-puller crumpled. Hellcat had found the tire iron.

They were exhausted, panting, bleeding, and shaking. Daniel lay on the slanted ground with head facing uphill. He probed at his face, trying to assess the damage. Hellcat dropped the tire iron near him and collapsed in a heap next to him. They heard the older woman's muffled yell come from inside the car. Daniel and Hellcat dragged themselves upright and staggered to it.

"Hang on! We'll get you out," Hellcat replied, her voice hoarse.

They edged up the sloping bank and tried to open the drivers side door, but the angles were wrong and gravity fought them. Daniel yelled through the closed window, "Can you hear me?"

They heard her muffled response, "Yes."

"We can't get the door open. We're going to break the window. Try to cover your face and head when I say so, okay?"

"Okay."

He found a large rock. It was tough moving on the slope while holding it with both hands, but with the young woman's help, he managed to get into position. He yelled, "Are you ready?"

"Ready."

Daniel smashed the large rock into the glass. It bounced off, having made only a few cracks. He tried again, and the spread through the safety glass like a crazy spider web. The window sagged inward a bit, nearly all of it still held in place. The third time was the charm. Hundreds of little pieces rained down on the older woman.

"You okay?" he asked.

"Yes, but please get me out of here."

Hellcat leaned through the opening. Daniel anchored her as she reached down past the steering wheel and stretched out her hands. "Here, Mom. Grab my hands."

"I can't move my right arm." The older woman weakly lifted her left arm, panting at the effort.

"I'll grab your hand, Mom. Don't try to grab mine." Their fingertips touched. The younger woman extended her stretch and grasped her mother's wrist with one hand and a few inches further up her arm with the other. "Got you! We'll take it slowly and help you to unwind."

It took a few minutes and multiple tries to figure out the best ways to get her head back up above her feet. Once that had been accomplished, her mother used her feet to help them lift her from the vehicle. Daniel and Hellcat each held one of the older women's hands to ease her the final few feet when Hellcat accidentally stepped on one of Daniel's feet in the dark. She slipped and instinctively grabbed for him, knocking him off balance. Neither let go of the older woman's hands as they fell, dragging her on top of them.

"Is this where I'm supposed to say thank you for breaking my fall?" the older woman wheezed.

The three burst out laughing as they untangled themselves and carefully edged away from the car, up the sloping bank, and then collapsed in a heap on the trail above, breathing hard.

The young woman said to Daniel when they'd caught their breath, "You're probably wondering how we got tangled up with those animals."

He smiled. "The thought had crossed my mind."

"Mom was taking me to the airport, when the car broke down. Smoke was coming from under the hood and the engine raced but we were slowing down. We pulled off to the side of the road to call for assistance, but our phones had no signal. Mom said that, about fifteen years ago, the same things happened with a different car and it turned out to be the transmission."

"Yes, back then I found I could still drive the car if I put it into first gear and kept the speed really low. That's where I got the idea to try the same thing tonight and drive down the trail to rescue my daughter."

Hellcat added, "We were discussing our situation when those animals showed up. We could tell they were trouble the moment we saw them. Thank you for stopping them."

"From what I saw, the two of you were putting up a hell of a fight before I came along."

"Fight or not, we were no match for them. We might not be alive if it weren't for you. Thank you." Hellcat stuck out a trembling hand "I'm Michelle, and this is my mom, Jean."

"Hi, I'm Daniel. Daniel Hansen," he said as they shook hands.

The women looked at each other and burst out laughing.

"Uh, did I say something funny?

Jean asked, "You wouldn't by any chance be on your way to meet Harrison Dunsmuir?"

Astonishment flashed on Daniel's face. "H-How'd you know that?"

"Harrison's my husband."

* * *

Less than ten minutes later, they heard the warbles and wails of a variety of emergency vehicles. It sounded as though a whole caravan of them were racing up the road above them.

They looked toward the sounds, and Daniel said, "What the…"

Michelle looked at Daniel, "Maybe we should try to run up there and flag them down."

She and Daniel wobbled to their feet, again needing to hold onto each other to keep from falling.

Jean Dunsmuir held up a hand, palm facing them. "Don't bother. They're moving too fast and we're too far from the clearing. You'd get there too late, even if you weren't exhausted and beat-up."

They looked at each other, nodded, and crashed into each other as they tried to sit back down. They burst into exhausted laughter.

Mrs. Dunsmuir continued, "Let's rest up a bit more before try to reach the clear…"

To their amazement, they heard the sound of air brakes. Colors from flashing lights and light from two bright beams penetrated the woods. The survivors yelled, "We're down here!"

An amplified voice asked, "Is anyone hurt?"

They looked at each other. Everyone was covered in blood, cuts, and bruises. They chuckled weakly when Michelle yelled in reply, "Everybody!"

They heard a stampede running down the trail toward them, and then saw flickers from the bouncing beams of flashlights.

Nearly a dozen emergency workers descended on them, using their flashlights to take in the scene. Two EMT's saw the shape they were in and rushed over to help them. One said, "We got you. Ambulances are on their way."

Daniel yelled to several deputies, "Four men attacked these women. Two are to the left of the car over there." He pointed in its direction. "Careful! It's teetering and could roll."

The senior cop, a sergeant, asked, "Where are the other two?"

"Down the trail a ways. The ones that are still alive are likely to be dangerous."

The sergeant turned to four of his team, "You heard the man. Get 'em." They split into two pairs and rushed off. The sergeant flashed his light onto the face of one of the unconscious men near the car. "Looks like the Barrett boys. They've been causing trouble all over these parts. Got rap sheets as long as my arm. We keep arresting them, and they keep being let go with slaps on the wrist. Based on what I see here, I think it's safe to say they'll be locked away for a long time."

Jean Dunsmuir said to the sergeant, "I know this may sound like a strange question, but why are you here? I mean, how did you know we needed help?"

He pointed to the taller mountain directly across the valley. "A Boy Scout troop was studying star constellations from Deane's Meadow over on Harris Mountain. They thought they saw a car drive off the road and crash through the woods. They reported it to a park ranger, who called it in. Based on where they were when they saw the accident, we figured it must've happened around here someplace. We knew for sure when we saw all the torn-up brush near the trail head. What happened?"

The trio began to tell their story…

＊ ＊ ＊

They healed quickly and well, with no lasting damage.

Soon after the three surviving Barrett boys got out of the hospital, they received twenty-year prison sentences. Daniel got the promotion. He and Michelle married a year later.

Over the mantel of their fireplace an ordinary-looking tire iron is proudly displayed. When visitors ask about it, Daniel and Michelle give each other a knowing look, smile, and say, "It's a long story."

Daniel never did see his father-in-law, The Dragon, spew fire.

Blood Oath

Although Jacob Makepeace was in his early forties, his face wore the wrinkles of a man aged beyond his years. Its pallor hinted of someone long denied sunlight. A trickle of sweat dripped down his forehead, stinging his eyes. He blinked rapidly, his eyes already irritated by too little sleep for too long. White lines rushed past, along with everything else he saw with his blurry eyes.

He stomped on the accelerator. The engine bucked and roared in protest, but complied, a wheeled horse jabbed by vicious spurs. Jacob looked at the clock on his dashboard for the hundredth time, willing it to move slower. *I can still reach her in time."*

He crested a hill and saw a jack-knifed gasoline tanker truck blocking the lanes. Its driver stood in the road, frantically waving his arms to get him to stop. Too late! Jacob hit the brakes, but the car was going too fast and swerved to the right. It crashed through a guardrail, plunged down a steep slope, glanced off a large tree, and somersaulted sideways before hitting a jagged boulder with a screeching blow. Atop the incline, a slow-motion chain reaction landslide followed the path the car had taken.

Jacob struggled to open his eyes, but blood joined the sweat and ran into them from a jagged gash in his forehead. He could barely see, even after repeatedly wiping it away with his shirt-sleeve. The trapped driver tried to move, but searing pain made him gasp and stop. His breathing was rapid and shallow. He looked down and saw his torso wedged between a bent steering column and compressed seat. He could tell by the excruciating pain and unnatural angles of what he could see of his legs that they were broken in multiple places. With his one good arm, he carefully felt around his rib cage and was met with sharp pain. *Must've busted some ribs too. Gotta get outta here. Get to Mary.* Mary. *Oh my God, what have I done?*

He smelled gasoline fumes. Their acrid odor strengthened. *The gas tank must have ruptured! Thank God, sparks didn't ignite it as we bounced down the cliff. But if something happens to Mary...* Soon fumes covered everything inside the car and liquid fuel pooled beneath the mangled cage that only moments before had been his only chance of reaching Mary in time.

Rocks the car had dislodged fell and crashed into a jagged boulder that dropped almost vertically for forty feet. It slammed into the car's rear quarter at just the wrong angle. Rock striking metal generated a spark that desperately sought fuel to keep living. It found that fuel in the gasoline fumes and morphed into an enraged monster of hellish flames that enveloped the trapped man. Jacob Makepeace could do nothing but try to protect his face with his one good arm. His screams echoed throughout the small canyons, reaching the ears of the helpless trucker who collapsed to his knees in horror.

Luke Barnett writhed in his bed, bathed in sweat. He jerked awake from a nightmare so real he could feel the heat of the flames and hear the man's screams. Somehow he knew the man in his dream was his father.

Luke lay there thinking, *What do I really know about him? He could have died many years ago or still be alive. I don't remember him at all. He left when I was a baby. Mom never said anything about him when I begged her to describe him. I don't even have a picture of him or know what he looked like. Heck, I don't know if he was tall or short, fat or thin.* For the ten-thousandth time, such questions swirled in his mind, but no answers came. The young man didn't notice that, for the first time, he posed those questions in the past tense.

Now Mom's dead and I'll probably never know about him. Her death yesterday had been as sudden as it was shocking. The police called it an accident, but he doubted it. His mom had been deathly afraid of heights, so afraid that she never ventured out onto the balcony of her tenth-story apartment. Luke also knew that she hadn't committed suicide. Only two days before her death, she'd told Luke how excited she was that her long-planned cruise to the Bahamas with her dearest friend was just two weeks away. He tried to convince the cops that she wouldn't have—*couldn't have*—committed suicide but they said there had been no indication of foul play and her neighbors hadn't heard anything suspicious.

Her death jarred him to the core. He planned to begin making funeral arrangements in the morning.

Now, this nightmare about someone he believed was his father stalked him. He decided to once again look for answers to the questions that haunted him.

Barnett was his mother's maiden name. Though he'd asked many times, no one would tell him the name of his father, nor had he ever met or even heard of any relatives on his father's side.

When Luke was twelve and his mother wasn't home, he discovered a possible clue as he snooped around looking for information. He found an old shoe box that had been shoved into a back corner of the top shelf of his mother's closet. The box contained a newspaper clipping, yellowed with age. On it was a name he'd never heard before: Jacob Makepeace. Luke copied every word of that clipping onto a piece of paper and carefully put everything back exactly the way he'd found it.

That distant memory drove Luke to go into the closet in his own room, pull down a shoe box from his shelf, and retrieve his hand-copied note. He smiled self-consciously at the immaturity of his handwriting. Luke laughed to himself when he realized he'd kept the note in his own apartment in nearly the same place his mother had: a shoe box in a closet. *Like mother like son, I guess.* The thought made his eyes mist over.

His mother had tried hard to raise him well despite the lack of a father's presence. Luke hung his head when he remembered how difficult he'd made her life during his rebellious years. Now, full-on tears streaked his cheeks. *I'm so sorry, Mom.*

Luke shook his head and blinked a few times to focus on the words he'd read and re-read so many times over the years:

"Jacob Makepeace was convicted of attempted murder of a law enforcement officer and sentenced to twenty years in prison."

Why would Mom keep this article? Could Jacob Makepeace be my father's name? He rolled the name "Makepeace" around in his mind as though tasting a flavorful food he hadn't had for along time. *Luke Makepeace. I like the sound of that. But why did he try to kill a cop? Was he framed? Maybe Jacob Makepeace isn't my father. Maybe she just somehow knew him, or was related to him. Too many questions and no answers!*

Frustrated, he carefully set the old page on his desk and threw the shoe box across the room. *What are you waiting for? You're old enough to find out about your own father! Now that Mom is gone, you won't even risk hurting her feelings. Maybe the search will even help me to find out what really happened to her.*

He knew how far-fetched that last thought was, but clung to the hope anyway. Luke decided to attempt to find the man and talk to him. It was getting late. He sighed. *Back to bed. Got a lot to do tomorrow.* He shook his head to try to clear away at least a little of the sadness. Before falling asleep, he began to make a mental list of the things he'd do in the morning.

Scratch-knock. He awakened with a jolt. *What was that?* Luke sat up in his darkened bedroom and listened. Knock …knock. *There it is again! Front door.* He reached for the lamp next to his bed, bumped it, and caught it before it could fall. He turned it on. Scratch…knock. Luke cursed under his breath and yelled: "Just a minute! I'm coming!"

He peeked at the clock and noted the late hour with disgust. *Who comes to the door so late at night?* He pulled on a pair of pants and stumbled to the front door. *Somebody better be dying!* He instantly regretted the thought when he remembered what had just happened to his mother.

With his hand on the doorknob, caution tempered his anger. Luke grabbed the baseball bat he always kept nearby and flipped the switch for the porch light, but it stayed dark outside. He peered through the peephole, but it was too dark to see anyone.

"Who is it?" He waited fifteen long seconds. No answer. "I said, *who is it?*" Still no answer. He cursed again under his breath. "Larry? This better not be another prank. I'm in no mood …"

He jerked the chain latch out of its slot and yanked open the door with his bat at the ready, white-knuckling it for dear life. Luke saw a man jump away from the light that suddenly streamed out of the entryway, as though the stranger had been scalded. The man remained in the shadows as he urgently whispered, "You Lucas Makepeace?"

Makepeace? The name in the article. The young man replied, "Sorry, mister. Wrong Luke. My last name's Barnett."

The stranger looked him over. "Ah, that's right, Barnett's your mother's maiden name. Your father paid someone to find you. He told me where you lived. I'm your father's friend. Please help me."

The man reached out a hand to make a pleading gesture. As it came into the light, Lucas instinctively pulled back. Blood covered the man's hand, which pressed against his abdomen.

Lucas hesitated. It could be all a lie or a scam, but curiosity overcame his concern. He leaned the bat against the wall—butted up against the door frame in easy reach—and helped the man inside and onto a couch.

The stranger began talking even before Lucas had a chance to close the door. His voice was deep, but weak. He spoke in a rush, stopping only to catch his breath. "I'm John Fenton. Your dad and I were friends in high school." He saw the still-open door. "Close and lock the door." Luke complied, and said, "You're badly hurt and should get to a hospital right—"

"No! They're hoping I'll do that, so they can finish the job." He pulled his bloody hand away from a jagged gash that began a few inches above his belt line. He quickly covered the wound again as blood seeped from it.

Lucas grabbed some clean towels and helped Fenton slow the bleeding. "I can't go to the hospital. Keg Crawford and his thugs will kill me. They already got your mother."

The news was a hammer blow to Lucas. *"What?"*

"I'd be dead, too, but saw 'em coming. Was getting in my car when Keg shot me." His breathing was getting faster but shallow. "Lost them in traffic. They won't stop 'til I'm dead."

"What about my father?"

"Died in a car crash yesterday on the way to your mom's. He'd called to warn her but couldn't get to her in time to save her."

Luke reeled, pressing a balled fist against his lips. He took fast, deep breaths, trying to hold himself together.

"We're all in danger." Fenton coughed, his breathing shorter. "Jennifer. You."

"Who's Jennifer?"

"My daughter."

"Daughter?"

Fenton nodded.

"How did all this start?"

"My family moved to another town when I was in my second year of high school. The new friends I made weren't like your dad. He was a straight arrow, the most loyal man I ever met. My new 'friends' and I were always getting into trouble. Your father kept trying to straighten me out. He never gave up on me. When he married your mother they both did all they could for me."

Pride welled up in Lucas. He'd longed to hear good things about his father all his life.

Fenton winced as he adjusted the makeshift bandage, and then continued, "I began doing drugs with those so-called friends. When the money ran low, I started gambling, desperate to win it back so I could buy more drugs. Jake—your father—tried to help me, tried to stop me. But I wouldn't listen."

Fenton shook his head sadly. "Got in way over my head. I missed a couple payments to Keg Clawson. He and about a half dozen of his thugs showed up at my place. Guess they figured that since I wasn't paying them they might as well use me to show others what happens to people that stiff Keg.

"They pulled me outside and started pounding on me. He wanted everyone to see. Probably knew any witnesses would be too scared to call the cops. Said they were going to break my kneecaps. Jake came from outta nowhere. Decked Keg and one of his gorillas. They pulled guns.

"Someone must've gotten up the nerve to call the cops. Keg's thugs started shooting at the first cops who arrived. Jake and I ran inside and tried to shut the door, but Keg and two of his goons began to push through. One got plugged in the back of the head and fell at our feet, blocking the door so it couldn't be closed. A lot more cops showed up. Keg's other thug made it inside with us and got plugged as he tried to clear the doorway and close the door.

"Keg aimed his gun at us, ordered us to clear the doorway, shut the door, and to pick up the guns of his downed men or he'd kill us. We knew he would and did what he said. We'd just grabbed the weapons when the cops rushed in and saw all three of us holding still-smoking guns."

Luke inhaled sharply and realized he'd been holding his breath.

Fenton continued, "Keg's gang wounded four cops and nearly killed one of them."

"Oh..."

"Yeah. We all threw down our guns and raised our hands. Keg yelled that we were trying to kill him. Cops didn't buy it." The wounded man sighed and bubbles of blood frothed at the corner of his mouth. "They didn't believe our story, either. They'd seen us holding guns that had just been fired and too much cops' blood had been spilled. They were out for blood and didn't seem too picky about whose they got. My arrest record didn't help. Since Jake was 'associating with known criminals,' they figured he'd recently joined the gang. I tried to tell them he was innocent and had just been just trying to save me, but Keg blamed us for the mess he was in, so he and his men claimed that Jake was as guilty as everyone else.

Luke exhaled sharply, the news another punch in the gut. He didn't know if he could take any more.

"We were all convicted of attempted murder of a cop. They wanted to keep us separate and sent us to three different prisons where we rotted for nearly twenty years. Keg still blames us for everything. Got word to us that he'd made a blood oath to kill us and our families when he got out."

Terror and rage burned white-hot inside Luke. He felt they were consuming him.

"Since we were convicted of the same crime. We all got out at about the same time. Since your dad had a clean record and no priors, he would have been released sooner, but Keg arranged for Jake to be framed for some other stuff while in prison to ensure Keg got out a little before the two of us. Not too much before, just enough. Must've had some help from some bent guards. Keg's prison was also closer to where your mom lived."

Luke didn't want to hear any more but knew he must. "Jake tried to call your mom, but she must have changed her number. Your dad died in a car accident as he raced to help her."

Luke silently took the steady blows, each burning away a little more of the innocent young man he'd been. He began to feel old, very old. Tears flooded his eyes. He let them fall. They slid down his cheeks and jaw, salty traces of his shattered life and heart.

The bleeding man continued, "When your mother opened the door of her apartment, Keg had just arrived there with four of his men. I walked out of the elevator about thirty feet away when they saw me. Keg pointed to two of his men and then to your mom. She was trying to get back inside when they grabbed her. One slapped a handkerchief over her mouth and clamped it down with his hand as the two men pushed her back inside. I *wanted* to help your mom. *Honest to God, I did!*" Tears began to fall from his exhausted, anguish-filled eyes.

Fenton clumsily clawed to wipe them away, as he continued, "Keg and two of his men came after me. They'd pulled their guns and had almost reached me. I had no choice but to run. I couldn't risk the elevator so I ran down ten flights of stairs and got away. No use getting the cops involved. I've been convicted of trying to kill a cop. They'd probably rather shoot than help me, and I've heard rumors that Keg's got some cops on his payroll.

Been running ever since and trying to warn my daughter Jennifer. She wasn't answering my calls. Finally tracked down her landlady. Said she's camping in an area with no cell phone reception. Burton Peak Wilderness Area. The landlady said she's there with two friends. Somewhere along Barrett Creek."

"I know that area. Spent a lot of time there. Isolated. Rugged."

"Was on my way to—" he gasped for air "—to find her. Realized I'd bleed out before I got there. Came here instead."

"We've got to warn her!"

"No! *You've* got to warn her." Fenton coughed. Blood dripped from his mouth. "I'll … be dead soon. Loss of blood or when Keg finds me."

Luke knew Fenton was right. The man was nearly dead already. It was getting harder for him to talk.

"Please find my daughter before they do. Please help her! I don't want her to die. I've been so stupid!" With great effort, Fenton pulled out his wallet and handed a photo to Luke. It was partially covered in blood from the wounded father's hand. Luke carefully wiped away the sticky red liquid. Friendly emerald green eyes and a stunning smile, long brown hair, a pert nose, and a few freckles greeted him.

"Beautiful, isn't she?" Fenton asked.

"Yes." Luke thought for a moment, and looked up from the photo. He almost blurted, "Maybe they won't find her," but knew it wasn't true.

"What if Jennifer doesn't believe me? I'm a stranger to her."

Fenton thought for a moment and then smiled. "When she was a baby, I used to tickle her nose with my eyelashes. She'd giggle. Her mom took a picture of me giving her those 'butterfly kisses.' She wrote to me that Jennifer loves that photo. Always keeps it on her nightstand. Tell Jennifer that knowing she did that helped keep me from going crazy all those years I was locked up."

After a moment, Luke asked, "What does Keg look like?"

"Big man. At least 6 feet, 3 inches. Blond hair. Before the shootout with the cops, your father broke Keg's nose. Gave him a gash over his right eye. When I saw Keg this morning, his nose still looked broken. He's got a jagged scar over his right eye." The memory made Fenton smile despite his pain.

Luke nodded, committing the visual to memory. "How will you protect yourself?"

"I brought a gun. Now, get out of here. Out the back way. Don't drive your car. Run. Call a cab when you get away. Pay cash. Got some?"

"Yes."

"Good! Take all the money you can. Here's what's left of mine." He pushed his wallet into the trembling young man's hands. "Go! Don't come back!"

Luke didn't know what to say, so he just nodded, stuck the dying man's wallet in his pocket, then grabbed money and his wallet from his bedroom. He quickly finished getting dressed.

Luke ran out the back door. He scrambled over the back fence and made it about one hundred feet down the street when the gunshots started. They didn't last long. He knew his father's best friend was dead, and now they'd be coming for him and a girl he'd never met but had to try to warn. A cold chill ran down his spine as anger consumed him. He ran as fast as he could, avoiding the glare of the streetlights.

Luke didn't need a cab. He called a buddy who worked nights only seven blocks away. Minutes later, Luke roared out of a park-

ing lot in a borrowed car headed for the wilderness and an unknown fate.

He knew Keg would find out from Jennifer's neighbors or
landlord where she'd gone. But the Burton Peak Wilderness Area
was huge. She could be anywhere. He hoped she kept to her plan
to stay somewhere near Barrett Creek. Maybe, knowing that, he
could find her first.

Along the way, he made a mental list of things he might
need. He remembered a store on the route that was a cross between a truck stop and sporting goods outfitter. It stayed open all
night for truckers, sportsmen, and other early morning travelers.
Luke ran in and grabbed each item on his mental list: headlamps,
two of the biggest knives he could find, rope, fishing line, and a
canteen. On his way out, he stopped at a water fountain and filled
the canteen.

Then Luke wondered if Burton's Peak had a ranger who
lived near the entrance of the park. He asked the clerk, "Does a
ranger live year-round at Burton Peak?"

"Yeah. George comes in all the time. Good guy. Gets most of
his supplies here."

"Happen to have his phone number?"

"Yup." He looked in an old folder of emergency numbers,
scratched a number on a scrap of paper, and handed it to Luke.

"Thanks!" Luke shouted as he ran out the door. He looked at
his watch: 2:07 a.m. He dialed the number and thought, *Ranger
George isn't going to be very happy with me.* The phone rang six
times. An irritated, raspy voice answered, "Burton Peak Ranger
Station. George Gorman here."

Luke explained the situation as fast as he could. At first, the
ranger thought it was a prank call, but, as the story unfolded, it
was soon clear the story was all too real.

"I saw the three young women you're talking about. They
said they planned to camp about seven miles up Barrett Creek.
That's nearly five miles beyond where the road ends. It's dark,
and the trail and terrain are treacherous. Only a fool would be
out walking around here tonight. Odds are that Keg fellow and

his gang are holed up for the night somewhere. Probably won't arrive until after daybreak."

Luke sighed with relief. "I hope you're right."

"To be on the safe side, I'll alert the sheriff. He'll probably have a bunch of deputies waiting for them when they arrive. Don't worry, son, we'll get them."

Luke allowed himself to feel hopeful for the first time since he answered the knock on his door. Was it only a few hours ago? It seemed like forever.

The ranger said, "Someone's knocking on the door. May be an injured camper. Stay on the line. I need more info from you. I'll be right back."

Luke started to yell a warning, but he heard the bump of the receiver being laid down. Then silence. Thirty seconds. *What's happening?* Then he heard two shots. Only two. He knew what had happened before the ranger's body hit the floor.

Luke hung up and called the sheriff's office as he raced for his car. The dispatcher didn't seem to take the ranting man seriously but said she'd send a patrol car to check on the ranger. She added, "We're in a big rural county and spread very thin. Although the closest deputy will get there as fast as he can it's going to take quite awhile to get there."

"That's too late. You better send a bunch of cars and an ambulance unless you want a dead deputy."

"Are you making a threat?"

Luke hung up. He wanted to run away and hide. But he knew Keg would find him just as he'd found the others. Besides, a woman's life was in danger, and probably the lives of the other two women with her. He'd just heard the murder of an innocent man, and he'd promised a dying man he would try to save Jennifer. Luke's mouth was so dry he couldn't even spit. With shaking hands, he rushed to the car and raced toward Burton Peak, determined to end this tonight.

A quarter mile from the ranger's home, he pulled into a fire trail and parked his car so it couldn't be seen from the main road. He headed into the woods toward the rear of the ranger's cabin.

The cabin was dark. He crept closer. A light flared in one of the back windows. Luke threw himself against a tree and froze. A moment later the light went out. Someone lighting a cigarette. No doubt one of Keg's men. Luke looked into the star-filled sky. He noticed with relief that the moon was only a sliver. *Good. Dark enough they probably won't see me if I try to get closer.*

He made it to the back wall of the cabin and pressed against it, the big knife in a shaking hand. He listened and heard two men talking.

"How long have Keg and the others been gone?" he heard a squeaky-voiced man ask.

"Only five minutes longer than the last time you asked. Quit asking!" came a gruff reply.

"I hope Keg kills her and gets back before dawn. Don't want anyone snooping around," said Squeaky Voice.

"Should be a snap. They're probably all sleeping. He'll pop all three of 'em with his silencer. Be back in plenty of time. Then we'll get that Makepeace or Barnett kid, or whatever he calls himself, so we can get on with our lives." Gruff voice.

Not if I can help it. Luke headed toward the Barrett Creek trail head.

It was dark. Too dark. Dangerous. He remembered Ranger George's words: "Only a fool would be out walking around here tonight." *Well, between Keg and his men, there are a lot of fools on this trail tonight, and I'm the biggest fool of all for trying to catch up to them.*

He needed light to see and to move fast. He hoped Keg and whoever might be accompanying him were far enough ahead and facing forward so they wouldn't see the red filtered light he used. The red light was much less visible at night than the white light of most flashlights. With luck, he'd see their white light before they'd see his red. It was a risk he'd have to take.

The trail grew increasingly steeper as it climbed. Luke knew from hiking it many times over the years, though never at night, that it was steep for most of the way and had a lot of hairpin curves. He was in pretty good shape and hoped that Keg and his city boys weren't. There was no reason to think any of them would be familiar with the trail or would suspect they were being followed. Both factors might slow them down and allow him to gain ground. He also knew a couple of short cuts. They were more treacherous, but could help him reach the women first.

He found one of the shortcut entry points. Good! It was sufficiently overgrown that the others would likely not have noticed it. Even if they had, they wouldn't know where it led and, he hoped, wouldn't have the confidence to leave the main trail.

When he reached the place where the second short cut began, Luke stopped for a moment and listened. He thought he heard something and killed his light. *There!* He saw flickering white lights perhaps five hundred yards down the trail. Five of them. He'd hoped there would be fewer. *Five men to kill three sleeping women. Overkill. With this shortcut, if I'm lucky I might reach the campsite ten or fifteen minutes ahead of them.*

Luke wondered how he'd awaken three sleeping women in the dark in the middle of nowhere without them screaming. If they screamed, Keg's men would hear it, and that would be the end of them. He came up with several scenarios but each seemed likely to lead to screams.

When the campsite came into view, the answer presented itself in the form of a short and sturdy redhead who had just crawled out of the tent. She probably had to pee. She walked in almost the opposite direction of where he stood. He waited until he heard her stop to do her business, then moved into position to intercept her as she walked back toward her tent.

NOW! He jumped her from behind, covered her mouth with his left hand, and wrapped his right arm around her, trapping her arms against her side. She started to struggle and tried to scream. He frantically whispered, "Shut up and listen. Five men are coming to kill Jennifer and all of you. They're just down the trail. No time to explain. You've got to trust me or we'll all die."

She answered by biting one of the fingers that covered her mouth so hard it bled. Luke grunted and nearly cried out in pain, but bit his lip instead.

Just then, both noticed a light far down the trail and heading their way. Then another, and another.

The redhead stopped struggling. He moved his hand slightly to allow her to whisper, ready to cover it again if she took a big breath to yell. "OK, maybe you're telling the truth, or maybe those are your friends," she said pointing to the lights creeping ever-closer. "How can I know you're telling the truth?"

"You can't. Jennifer can. Wake up your friends quickly and quietly. I'm trying to save you, not kill you! Tell them to bring their coats, shoes, and flashlights. Leave everything else. Hurry!"

The redhead ran to the opening of the tent. He heard urgent whispering. Three terrified women emerged. He went to the only brunette and said, "Jennifer, your dad said to tell you about the butterfly kisses he gave you as a baby and the photo your mom took of your dad giving you a butterfly kiss that's on your nightstand."

Jennifer nodded in recognition, eyes wide with fear. "Is Dad okay?"

"No time to talk." He pointed at the lights bouncing along the trail. You three head up the trail. Do you know where the trail forks to the left near Barrett Creek about a quarter mile from here?"

"Yeah, at William's Overlook."

"Beneath the overlook is a deer trail. Follow it. When it peter's out, take the next deer trail that veers right. After about a mile it should intersect with the main trail. Don't go to your car or the ranger's cabin. He's dead. Two of Keg's men are hiding there in case you slip past Keg or someone calls on the ranger before Keg is off the mountain. Flag down anyone who is alone in a car. Get to the county sheriff. Go now!

"What about you?"

"I know the trail. I'll try to slow them down. Give you more time."

Her emerald eyes, their color masked by the night's darkness, looked deeply into his as she whispered, "Thank you." Then the women rushed away.

The women were gone only about two minutes when the first two of Keg's men arrived. They looked exhausted. Then Keg showed up, followed shortly later by two others who were panting hard. They wasted no time surrounding the tent. Keg screwed on the silencer to the barrel of his gun. Un-silenced gunshots might be heard for many miles and draw unwanted attention. On his signal, they all aimed their flashlights through the tents thin material onto the sleeping bags. Keg quickly shot through the tent, emptying his clip into them. The men cheered.

"Shut up!" he hissed. "Something's wrong!" Keg growled. He pulled a switchblade from his pocket, slashed through the side of the tent, and shook the sleeping bags.

"Where are they?" he growled, his face crimson. He felt the bags again. "They're still warm! They must have just left. Couldn't have gone far."

"Maybe they heard us coming." One of his men guessed.

"Ya think?" Keg sneered. Well, they are only three unarmed women, and there are five of us with guns."

The men nodded and smiled. Piece of cake.

"They didn't slip past us on the trail." He pointed to a sheer cliff jutting straight up on one side of the trail and a steep drop-off on the other. Both could be seen extending at least five hundred yards down the trail they'd just come up, and quite a ways above them. That meant their prey had only one way to go. He turned to point to the trail heading above them when they saw a brief flicker of white light in that direction.

"There they are. We've got 'em, boys. Capture 'em alive. Gonna have some fun with 'em. Make 'em wish they'd never been born! Then we'll kill 'em."

Seventy feet up the trail and behind a big tree, Luke saw and heard it all. He rushed further up the trail, which became so steep that he was panting before long. He knew the out-of-shape men below him would be even more worn out. A plan formed in his mind. Luke needed the distance between the men to increase. He had no chance against five armed men bunched closely together, but, if he could spread them out, he just might be able to get one or two—and maybe one of their guns—and slow the others down before they got him.

He needed to buy time. He had no illusions as to what would be his fate. The odds against him were simply too high and his options too few and almost all bad.

The steep slope and darkness were his allies. He found a perfect spot for an ambush. The trail continued upward nearly straight for about thirty feet and followed a cliff with a steep drop-off on the right side. Then the trail veered sharply left. He tied thick fishing line about four inches above the base of a tree immediately across from where the trail formed a sharp "V" next to the trail then let it sag to the ground, lightly sprinkled dirt over it, and unspooled it in the straight line on the left side of the trail that began just before the V.

Thirty feet down-trail he wrapped the line around a large tree and hid behind it. He found a big flat rock he could easily handle. Luke breathed slowly and quietly. He let one man walk past him, then another, and then Keg. He didn't like letting any of those men get between him and the women, but it was necessary to have any chance for his plan to work.

The men were spread out, roughly forty feet apart. A fourth man trudged past him, panting. Luke grabbed a flat rock. About twenty seconds later, number five hurried abreast of the tree Lucas hid behind. *Now!* He hit the man on the back of the head so hard the rock split in two. Lucas heard the crunch as the skull caved in and the man folded like a rag doll. One down. Luke hoped to have time to find the man's gun, but the fourth man heard the noises behind him. He yelled to the men ahead and started racing toward Number Five. He remembered the sharp curve in the trail and had just begun to slow down as he neared the V when Luke pulled up on the fishing line from his position behind the tree thirty feet down-trail. Number Four never saw it coming. He tripped and fell over the cliff. His panicked scream lasted for two seconds and then abruptly stopped, the only evidence of his existence there was faint echoes bouncing off distant canyon walls.

Luke didn't stop to listen to them. He raced back to Number Five, felt around for the man's gun, grabbed it, and patted the man's pockets. *There!* He pulled out an extra ammo clip and pocketed it just as a bullet ricocheted off a tree inches from his head. There wasn't enough cover for the next two hundred feet down-trail. He had to make his stand right here. Three against one. Out-manned and out-gunned. They also probably had a lot more ammo—and experience. Odds were, this was going to end very badly. Luke hoped he'd buy Jennifer and her friends enough time to get away.

Keg and his men began shooting at him from behind trees and boulders.

Luke tried to conserve ammo, but he couldn't let them flank him or get closer. Then he pulled the trigger and heard a sickening click. Empty! They heard it, too.

Keg yelled, "Rush him! I'll cover you."

Luke frantically ejected the empty clip and inserted his only replacement. He reached around the tree and pulled the trigger just in time to drop a man who was only five feet from him. He turned to take a shot at another man who had been three steps slower, but his target jumped behind a tree and the bullet meant for him ricocheted away.

Keg saw Luke's exposed arm and pulled the trigger three times in rapid succession. Searing pain traveled up Luke's arm with such intensity that Lucas dropped his gun. He desperately tried to pick it up, but his right arm and hand wouldn't work. He grabbed the gun with his left hand firing just in time to wing Keg's only remaining man. The man went down but kept firing. Every time Luke fired, he knew it might be his last bullet. Then it happened. That sickening click. It was all over now.

Keg stood up with a triumphant smile. Then he shrieked. His head jerked sharply backwards, accompanied by a terrible crunching noise. Jennifer stood over the collapsing man, holding the blood-stained, wedge-shaped rock she'd used to break his neck from behind.

Keg's remaining man turned to shoot Jennifer, but saw Sue out of the corner of his eye, wielding a log like a club. He aimed his gun at her. Too late. She smashed her makeshift club into his gun hand and sent the weapon flying. Yelling in pain and fury, he lunged for the gun. She bashed him on the head. He crashed to the ground unconscious.

When he came to he was tied up to a tree, bandaged arm in a sling.

Jennifer bandaged Luke's injured arm and said, "Just a flesh wound."

"A damned painful flesh wound, if you ask me," Luke smiled, then winced as the dressing was tightened to help staunch the loss of blood. "Why did you come back? You could have gotten away."

Jennifer shrugged. "Wendy sprained her ankle. We couldn't leave her and couldn't outrun the men. We heard the shooting and knew you needed help. You risked your life to save ours. The least we could do was return the favor."

The 'Misunderstanding'

The trip had been grueling. Like practically everyone else crowded around the luggage carousel, Tim Johnson was tired and getting impatient. Watching the endless stream of suitcases, he marveled again at the similarity of the bags: Most were black and in similar shapes and sizes. He thought, *Why do so many people buy bags that look like all the others?* He laughed at the irony, realizing he included himself among those people. *At least most people are smart enough to put a colored ribbon on them, so they can more quickly find theirs.* For this trip, Tim had used ribbons with a print of miniature playing cards on them for his bags. He found Evelyn's bag and the one with drawings of playful puppies and kittens on it that belonged to their five-year-old daughter Grace. *Now where's mine? Ah, there it is!* He saw the playing cards on the ribbon and grabbed it as his wife called to him:

"Jayce and Vickie are nearly out front. Let's go before they have to drive around the airport again." Lugging his family's baggage, Tim joined his wife and daughter as their long-time closest friends, the Kendalls, pulled up to the curb. After brief hugs and greetings, they loaded the luggage into the Kendalls' vehicle. Stories about their daughter's first trip to Disneyland filled the drive home.

The Kendalls helped unload the baggage and said goodnight. As their taillights receded, the phone in the Johnsons' house rang. Tim muttered, handed off sleepy, four-year-old Grace to Evelyn, fumbled for his keys, and barely reached the phone before the fifth ring would have sent the caller to the answering machine. "This is Tim."

"Tim Johnson?"

"Yes."

"*You stole my bag and I want it back!*"

"What are you talking about?"

"At the airport! You're dead if you opened or took anything from it!"

"Whoa! I don't take kindly to threats. You want to calm down?"

"No! I want my suitcase!"

"Hang on a minute. Did you have a ribbon tied to it?"

"Yeah. A ribbon with playing cards."

"Uh oh, I tied the same kind of ribbon on mine. Hang on. Let me check. What's your name?"

"Billy Burdett. Yeah, go check, *but you better not open it!*"

Tim set the phone down, grabbed the suitcase, checked the name on the ID tag, and sighed.

"I have your bag. I'm sorry. I must have taken yours by mistake. Do you have mine?"

"Yes."

"How'd you get our phone number? We didn't put it on the address tag."

"I found an address book in your suitcase. Started calling people until someone gave it to me."

"At this time of night? And you searched through our bag? What gave you the right—"

"*Shut up! I want my bag!*"

Tim looked at the clock on the wall and shook his head. "It's late. I'll be happy to meet you at the airport tomorrow morning to swap our bags."

"No. *I'm comin' now!* Remember, you're dead if you open it." The line went dead.

Tim held the phone a moment, trying to fight back panic and figure out what to do. "Evelyn, take Grace to the Harrisons' and stay there."

"Why? What's wrong?"

"Some nut job is coming here. I accidentally grabbed his bag at the airport. He made threats. It's probably nothing, but just in case, I want the two of you out of the house when he comes."

"Call the cops."

"Do you really think we need to?"

"Call the cops, please."

"I will, as soon as you're both safe. Hurry."

"Come with us."

"No. If I go, it'll just make him madder. I want this resolved tonight. Don't worry, the cops will probably get here before he does."

Evelyn scooped up Grace, and saw the concerned look on the girl's face. "It's okay, dear. We accidentally got the wrong suitcase at the airport and Daddy's going to wait here to give it back to him when he comes for it. You and I are going to your friend Mara's house to visit. Okay?" Grace smiled and nodded. "Give Daddy a kiss goodbye." Tim bent down and kissed the two most precious people in his life. He opened their front door and stepped outside to look around. Reassured, he nodded to his wife. She looked into his eyes and pleaded, "Be careful."

"I will."

Tim watched until they were safely inside the neighbors' house, and then called 911. When his call was answered, he said, "My name is Tim Johnson. I'm at my home at 2735 Beekman Street. A very angry man named Billy Burdett whom I've never met just telephoned to say he was coming over right now, and he threatened to kill me. He sounds crazy. I fear for my life. I have a loaded gun and don't want to hurt anyone but I will defend myself. Please hurry!" It was all true, and Tim knew that police tended to quickly respond to such calls.

He went to his gun safe, but his hands were shaking and it took a couple of tries to unlock it. Tim pulled out and loaded five rounds of buckshot into his 12-gauge pump shotgun, and six .357 Magnum rounds into his Ruger Blackhawk revolver. He didn't want trouble, but this wacko scared him. Tim wanted to be prepared and able to defend himself. He wasn't a great shot, but, with a shotgun at close range, he wouldn't miss no matter how scared he was.

Tim brought Burdett's bag to the front door and jotted down the man's name and address in case he left before the cops arrived. He placed the guns so they'd be out of sight but within reach. *Come on, cops! Get here!*

BANG-BANG! Battering ram-level pounding assaulted his door and eardrums. He jumped when it started, as his mind and heart raced. *Where are those cops? Do I answer the door or try to talk to him through it and stall him until they get here. How much more of a beating can that door take?*

"I'm here, piss-ant! Open up! Give me my bag or I'll break down your door and then ring your scrawny neck!"

A couple of police cruisers screeched to a halt, and two cops rushed to the front door. Tim watched through the peephole and could hear through the door. Burdett looked huge, probably weighing nearly as much as the two cops combined. But the tone and demeanor of the furious man immediately changed as soon as they arrived. Now he was acting friendly and deferential. The perfect innocent, law-abiding citizen. "Good evening, officers."

The older of the two officers asked, "What's going on here?"

"Oh it's nothing really. Just a little misunderstanding. This Johnson fella and I accidentally took each other's bags at the airport. When I tried to get mine, he threatened me." Burdett knocked again, this time gently. Tim opened the door and the suitcases were quickly exchanged.

"He was the one who threatened—" Tim spluttered.

"STOP!" The taller cop cut him off. "It's one man's word against the other, so I'm warning both of you: this better be the end of it. You both have your own bags back. No more threats from either of you. Do you both understand?"

Burdett smiled, nodded and said, "Certainly, officer." Tim felt the heat rise in his face and was so furious he could barely speak, but managed to say, "Okay."

Burdett asked, "Can I go now?"

"Yeah."

Burdett looked at Tim, smiled, and said, "Sorry for this little misunderstanding." Then he picked up his suitcase, turned and left.

"May we come in, Mr. Johnson?"

"Yes, of course." Tim noticed the three stripes on the older cop's sleeves, and motioned toward a couch in the living room. "Please have a seat, sergeant, and officer, uh..."

The younger cop filled in the blank: "Trowden."

As Tim led them into his home, the sergeant looked around and noticed Jim's guns; the handgun lying on a table near the door, and the shotgun tucked in the crook made by the table and the wall. He turned to the younger officer behind him and signaled with his head toward the guns. Trowden saw them and nodded.

When the cops were seated, Tim selected a chair across from them and sat. "Thank you for coming so quickly."

The older cop nodded in acknowledgment. "I'm Sergeant Murphy. On the way here we checked the record of the man you said threatened you. William Jason Burdett aka 'Billy' has a long rap sheet. Mostly violent crimes. Been in and out of prison. To our knowledge, he hasn't done anything lately and isn't wanted for anything. We could have brought him downtown, but since it was your word against his, he'd probably be released before we walked back to our patrol cars. And he'd probably be angrier than ever. Burdett is a violent and vengeful man. The type who tends to hold grudges a long time. Maybe our warning scared him off, but, just in case, I'll request extra patrols on your street for a while."

"Thank you, Sergeant."

The cops stood and headed toward the front door. Tim got there first and held it open for them. Murphy stopped about two feet from Tim, locked eyes with him and warned, "Be careful with this guy. He's dangerous and doesn't make idle threats. Keep your house locked and call us right away if he contacts you again."

"Will do." Tim let out a big breath as he closed and locked the door behind them. He leaned against it to process all that had happened.

A minute later, he heard someone try to turn the doorknob. Instinctively Tim grabbed it with his left hand to keep the doorknob from turning as his right hand snatched the stock of the shotgun. *Knock-knock*. Through the door he heard the voice of the woman with whom he planned to spend the rest of his life with. "Hey it's me. Open up. It's cold out here, and Grace is getting heavy." Tim burst out laughing, relieved at the sound of Evelyn's voice.

"Sorry. Just a sec, hon." He set the shotgun back in its nook and unlocked and opened the door. Evelyn rushed in, Grace asleep in her arms, whispered words flying rapidly. "What happened? Wait! Let's first put Grace to bed." She carried their golden-haired treasure to bed. Tim tucked her in, and they kissed her forehead. The couple looked at each other with proud smiles, made sure the night light was on, shut off the light, and closed her door.

Evelyn began again the moment they were out of earshot from Grace. "Okay, tell me everything." Before Tim could open his mouth to say a word, she kept going. "Are you all right? I saw the man leave and then the cops leave. He threatened you! Why didn't they arrest him?"

Tim held up a hand. "Whoa. Let's sit down. I'll tell you everything. Drink?"

She nodded, impatience in her eyes.

"Wine?"

"Yes."

"Which?"

"Anything! Now, would you please tell me what happened?"

"Fine! Have an apple." He took one out of a fruit bowl and handed it to her with a mischievous smile on his face. She grabbed it and threw it at him, but missed his head by a foot. It bounced off some drapes onto the floor and under a table. "C'mon. I'm serious. Quit teasing me!"

Tim reached under the table, picked up the bruised fruit missile, and put it on top of the bowl's contents. He mused, "You used to be a better shot."

Evelyn knew her husband used levity to help them calm down and relieve some tension. But enough was enough. "Timothy Joseph Johnson! She hissed.

He told her everything, careful to make Burdett sound bad enough that she'd be careful and concerned, but not so bad that she'd be petrified.

Tim said, "I think that's the last we'll hear of him. The cops probably scared him away."

Evelyn didn't look convinced, so he added, "I'll install a chain lock on the front and back doors."

"I want a home security system."

"Okay."

"I'll call someone tomorrow."

"Sure, hon."

Evelyn added, "How about a big watchdog?"

"Well, maybe we should hold off on that for a bit. Grace is still pretty small. Let's go to bed, I'm exhausted."

"Please lock up the guns first."

Tim was torn about what to do about the guns. He wanted to leave one out, loaded, and within reach so he'd be able to defend his family if that Burdett creep came back; but, with a young child in the house, he'd promised Evelyn years ago to keep his weapons locked in the safe when they were in the house. He knew she was right. One look at her pursed lips and crossed arms made it clear she there would be no room for discussion on the matter. Tim nodded, unsuccessfully tried to stifle a yawn, stood up, stretched his exhausted body, and put the guns away. He left them loaded.

He locked the doors and left the front porch light on. During his before-bed bathroom routine, his mind kept flashing back to the huge angry man who had been at his front door. The insults and threats. The man's vicious rage over a simple, innocent mix-up. Tim marveled at how Burdett was able to turn that all off in an instant and act pleasant and normal when the cops arrived. *He must be a psychopath or sociopath. What's the difference between the two? Are they the same? Is one a subset of the other? I think I remember hearing that about one percent of the general population is psychopathic, but the ratio quadruples or more among people in powerful roles.* His mind continued wandering. He tried to envision Burdett in a big business suit as the CEO of a major corporation, but the image was so ludicrous that he burst out laughing. He swallowed some of the toothpaste in the process, which made him cough. He sprayed a mouthful of the minty mess onto the mirror and faucets, and into the sink. Tim looked at his reflection in the foam-splotched mirror. Light-blue speckled foam dribbled down his chin. He laughed, spluttering some more as he tried to collect himself.

Tim cleaned up the mess and crawled into bed. He could tell by Evelyn's breathing she was already asleep. He figured he was so exhausted he, too, would quickly fall asleep. Tim was wrong. His mind dwelled on the threats the big man had made. Now that Burdett had what he wanted, would that be the end of it? Tim's gut didn't think so, and it kept him up for hours worrying about it. Burdett's eyes haunted him. If the eyes were truly windows to the soul, then Burdett had no soul. His eyes were cold, bottomless pits of darkness. *Pull yourself together! You're probably worrying over nothing.* When he finally fell asleep, nightmares of the big man began where his conscious mind had left off.

Someone was shaking Tim's shoulder. "Tim! Wake up! Did you hear that?" *Evelyn.*

"Unh? Huh? Hear what?" Tim opened his eyes. It was still dark.

"I heard something break in the front yard!"

Adrenaline surged, waking Tim instantly. "What did it sound like? Breaking glass? A window?" They turned on their bedside lamps almost simultaneously.

"I don't know. Maybe."

Tim saw Evelyn's cell phone on top of the bedside table. The clock next to it read 4:33 in its usual eerie red glow. "It's probably nothing, but I'll go check. To be on the safe side, bring Grace in here and lock the door. If I'm not back in two minutes, call 911." Tim grabbed a flashlight from the drawer of his nightstand. It had a long reinforced handle and was built solidly, the kind that could be used as a club in a pinch. He headed for the front door.

She whisper-yelled after him as she headed for Grace's room. "Be careful!"

"I will. It's probably nothing." *Please let it* be *nothing. Damn, I wish I had my shotgun right now. No time to get it.*

Tim reached the front door and peered through the peephole. The porch light was still on. His vision was limited to the bubble the peephole and light offered, but he saw nothing out of the ordinary. Tim unlocked the door, took a big breath, swung the door wide open, waited a moment to see if anything jumped at him, and then rushed through the door with the "club" at the ready. Shocking cold immediately assaulted his bare feet, and the wind reminded him that he was only clad in an undershirt and sleeping shorts. Tim began shivering. He was glad it wasn't the middle of winter, but it was still plenty cold.

Tim aimed the flashlight's beam in wide arcs, but didn't see anyone. He tried to ignore the cold and hoped the neighbors didn't see him half-dressed like this.

A thought struck him as he switched his search for signs of broken window. *I'm in bare feet looking for broken glass in my under-wear in my front yard in the middle of the night.* He stepped more slowly and carefully, alternating the level of the beam between window height and the area in front of his feet. All the windows in the front part of the house were intact. He was about to head back inside when the very edge of the beam illuminated an empty space where a pot full of flowers had rested on a narrow brick window ledge. He found the clay pot thirty inches beneath the now-vacant spot. It lay shattered on the cement lawn mow-strip, its flowers smashed and scattered among the wreckage.

Tim breathed a long sigh of relief, ran back inside, and closed and locked the front door behind him. He bathed in the warmth that enveloped him as he walked to their bedroom door. Tim rapped quietly, not wanting to wake Grace. He whispered, "It's okay. It's me." Evelyn opened the door with one hand as she held their sleeping daughter in her other arm, cellphone cradled between her cheek and neck.

Tim said, "The wind or a cat must have knocked one of the clay flower pots off a window sill. Let's get Grace back to bed."

Evelyn spoke quietly into her phone. "False alarm. Sorry to bother you."

Forty feet away, in the darkness just outside the lit area of the porch light near where a forlorn heap of potting soil, clay shards, and broken flowers lay, was the imprint of a shoe worn by a very big man.

* * *

A week passed. Tim installed the chain lock, and Evelyn ensured the security alarm system was installed. They agreed to hold off getting a watchdog until Grace was a little bigger. They wanted to research the best breeds for family dogs that were good with kids but big enough to be good watchdogs. Daily routines and responsibilities helped make the "Burdett incident" begin to fade from their minds.

One bright morning after Tim left for work, Evelyn opened their automatic garage door and loaded Grace into her car seat in the back of their sedan. As she stood up, a hand grabbed her hair and yanked her around. Evelyn cried out in pain and fear. She was looking at the lower part of the chest of a huge man. He thrust his hulking frame against her so hard she gasped and crashed against the car's door frame.

"*Mommy!*" Grace screamed and began sobbing.

The man clamped a massive hand over Evelyn's mouth, leaned down and brushed his lips against her ear. She felt his hot breath and the rough whiskers of a week-old beard. His voice was deep and gravelly, but he whispered so softly she had to strain to hear. "Make a sound and she dies. Understand?" She quickly nodded. He unclamped her mouth.

Evelyn turned her head toward her child and tried to sound reassuring but was so upset her voiced wavered. "It's okay, honey. This man and I are just ... talking." Evelyn turned back to face the massive man.

The brute whispered, "Got a message for your piss-ant husband: Tell him I tried to settle this man to man, but he called the cops. If he does it again, I'll kill all three of you. Slowly. After he watches me use you in very painful ways. Understand?"

Burdett rubbed his rough hand against her face. "Tell him he'll see me again. Soon."

He slapped her face so hard, it felt on fire. Her ears rang and blood trickled from her nose. "That's a love tap compared to what I'll do to you and your girl if the cops are called again." He laughed, a wicked laugh that got louder and deeper as he walked away.

✳ ✳ ✳

Jayce Kendall answered his home office phone. "Hello?"

"It's Tim. That psychopath I told you about last week just attacked Evelyn in our garage. He threatened to kill her and Grace if I call the cops again. She's nearly hysterical. I'm headed home, but I'm at least thirty minutes away."

"I'm closer and will be there in ten."

"Thank you!"

"Thank you!" Jayce heard some relief in his friend's voice, but mostly panic. He'd never heard his friend so worried. "Bring a gun. This guy is huge. And violent."

"Okay. I'm on my way. Try to calm down. It won't help them if you get killed racing to get home."

Jayce hung up before his friend could respond. He grabbed his Glock .40 S&W as he ran to his car. The weapon was already loaded with hollow point rounds known for stopping what they hit.

Jayce got to the Johnsons' house in less than eight minutes, parked out front, and rushed to the front door. He got out, jammed his weapon under his belt at the small of his back, and rushed to the front door. He tried the door knob and was relieved that it was locked. He shouted, "Evelyn, it's Jayce. Open up!"

The door flew open and Evelyn flew into his arms. "Thank God, it's you."

Jayce returned the hug and moved them both inside. He closed and locked the door behind them. As they stood in the entryway, he leaned back to get a look at her. Dried blood still streaked her face from her bloody nose. A bright red image of a giant hand still showed from the bottom of her chin to the top of her left ear. She talked so fast he couldn't understand her.

"Whoa, slow down a bit. He led her to the couch. "Let's sit down and talk." She sat. "But first I'll get you some water. Be right back."

Jayce returned momentarily with a large glass of water and a wet towel. He handed the glass to her and said, "Here, take a drink." He sat down next to her.

He sat down next to her. Evelyn nodded her thanks as she took the glass and gulped the water down as though she'd been lost in a desert for days without water.

"Better slow down a bit, Evelyn."

The brunette came up for air and set the nearly empty glass down on an end table. "Thank you!"

"You okay?"

"I am now, but I've never been so scared in my life."

"You're safe now, and Tim's on his way. Where's Grace?"

"A friend's mom took her to nursery school. I called in sick to work."

"Good. Let me see your face." He gently touched her chin with his left hand and used the wet towel to wipe away as much of the blood as he could with soft swipes.

"OOH!"

"Sorry. I'm trying to be as gentle as I can."

"I know. And thank you."

"Tell me what happened."

Evelyn had just finished telling Jayce the story when Tim arrived. Jayce unlocked and unchained the door, and let him in. Evelyn jumped up and rushed to her husband. They held each other in a tight embrace.

Jayce had calmed Evelyn down, but Tim was livid. When he was sure Evelyn and Grace were okay, and his wife had lain down to rest, he motioned for Jayce to join him in his den and closed the door.

Before his friend could say what was on his mind, Jayce said, "We should take photos of the blood and bruises on Evelyn's face as evidence of Burdett's attack for the police."

"No! The police admitted they've already arrested him for violent crimes and the system lets him off over and over again. Even if he were sent to prison, they wouldn't keep him there for very long. They said Burdett is a violent and vengeful man and the type who holds onto grudges for a long time. My family will never be safe as long as he's alive. I'm going to have to track down and kill that son of a bitch! My family won't be safe until he's dead!"

"That's what he *wants* you to do so he can ambush you on his turf. That way, when he kills you, it will be self-defense. Plus, think about your family."

"I *am* thinking about them!"

"No. I mean, even if you kill him, you'll end up in prison for murder. How will going to prison help them?"

Tim's whole body shook as he brought clenched fists to his chest and his head sank. A moment later his head slowly raised. His eyes bored into Jayce's with burning ferocity as he snarled, "What do you *want* me to do? Wait until he kills me and my family?"

"No. I want you all to stay with Vickie and me for a couple days. These things have a way of working themselves out."

Tim doubted that anything would fix the mess he was in, but he agreed to stay at the Kendall's.

Jayce said, "I'll call Vickie to let her know what's going on. You and Evelyn go pack enough stuff to stay for a week. We'll pick up Grace on the way to my house."

Twenty minutes later the Johnsons were in their car leading their friend in his car as they headed to Grace's nursery school. Jayce vigilantly looked at his three mirrors to make certain they weren't being followed.

* * *

Billy Burdett lived in a secluded trailer at the end of a poorly maintained dirt road. He sat on a threadbare recliner and watched his third game of the day. He drained the last bottle of the twelve-pack he'd bought earlier that afternoon and went to the kitchen to see if any strays were hiding in a back corner of the refrigerator. He pushed things around and came up empty-handed. He kicked the fridge.

"Damn it!"

He heard a knock on the side of his trailer. He growled, clenched his fists, walked over and opened the trailer door, snarling, "Who is it and waddya want?"

Burdett looked around, but didn't see anyone. He cursed and was about to close it when a man shouted from the other side of Billy's old yellow pickup truck. The big man grabbed the baseball bat he kept near his door and stormed out. Halfway there, a man stepped out of the shadows and stood about four paces in front of him. Burdett stopped, banged his bat with one hand into his other so hard and loudly it would have made an ordinary man wince in pain. "Who the hell are you and waddya want?"

"I'm the man who's going to make sure you never bother Tim and Evelyn Johnson again."

Burdett's laughter came out a roar. He took a step toward the intruder, relishing the pain he was about to inflict. "You and what army?"

"This one." Jayce whistled. Eighteen men stepped out of the darkness, creating a circle around Jayce and the huge brute. Each wielded a tire iron, axe handle, length of chain, or length of metal pipe.

. "Funny you should mention "army." These are some of my friends from our Army Reserve unit."

Burdett stopped dead in his tracks and closed his mouth so tightly that Jayce could see the twitching of his jaw muscles. The brute slowly turned to see what he was up against. He knew he could take out several of them but not all of them. Suddenly, as though a switch had been flipped, his tone and demeanor became downright friendly. "I think there must be some misunderstanding."

Jayce smiled, and said, "Yeah, Tim told us you'd probably say that."

Silence.

Jayce turned his head to the right and yelled toward the shadows. "Hey, Tim. Got a minute?" Tim showed himself and walked into the circle to stand next to his friend. Jayce continued, "Well Burdett, you have exactly one chance to correct this 'misunderstanding' by confessing everything you did and apologizing to Tim for it."

"Hell no. I'm not sayin'—"

"That was your chance!" Twenty men moved as one toward Burdett.

"Wait!"

The men stopped.

Burdett pursed his lips, then spoke, "Okay. I threatened you and your family."

"And grabbed my wife's hair, slammed and trapped her against her car, and slapped her so hard she got a bloody nose and huge bruise on her face."

Burdett looked at the men in the circle looking for lack of resolve or weakness. All he saw was determination. Several smiled.

Billy whispered, "Yes."

"What was that?"

"*Yes!* I'm sorry! Okay?"

"And threatened to rape her and our little girl, and kill all of us."

"Now wait a minute, I didn't…"

The circle of men tightened further.

"Okay. Yes. I threatened to do all those things."

"What things?"

Seething, Burdett confessed, "I threatened to rape your wife and daughter in front of you and then kill you all, you piss-ant. Why don't you just come here and we'll settle it man to man?"

The circle of closed so tightly the men's shoulders touched.

Once again, the brute's tone and demeanor instantly changed. "Okay! I'm sorry, and I promise to leave you and your family alone."

Jayce laughed, "You're not getting off that easy." Several men pulled out their phones and played back Burdett's confessions. "We have the evidence to give to the cops that along with your priors could get you put away for years."

"No! Wait! You look like reasonable men. There must be another way." He used his best pleading voice, the one that convinced judges and juries. It had sometimes even worked with the more gullible among them. "I'll be good this time, I promise."

Jayce offered, "Well, there is another option, one that would save us taxpayers a lot of money in a lengthy trial, plus all those prison costs."

"What is it?"

"We all decided the climate here is bad for your health. It's time you left the state and never came back. Tonight."

"*What?*"

The circle of men tightened a bit further, now two tight rings one just inside the other and getting perilously close to him.

"*Okay!* I'll go."

Tim stared straight at him, nodded, and said, "If that's what you really want."

Burdett growled, "It is."

"Okay. You've got thirty minutes to clear out."

Burdett headed for his trailer. Several men stayed with him to make sure he didn't try anything. Some others helped him to move some of his bigger stuff into his truck.

On a hunch, Jayce searched the old pickup while Burdett was in the trailer. He found a loaded large caliber revolver under the driver's seat and pocketed it. The world and his friends would be safer if Burdett didn't have it.

Twenty-seven minutes after Burdett started packing, he was in his truck and ready to go.

"To make sure you don't get lost, these men will follow you 'til you cross the state line. Then we'll turn your confession over to the cops." If you decide to come back, either the cops will get you or we will. You better hope it's the cops. Understand?"

Burdett nodded, but hatred burned in his eyes. He floored the old beat-up yellow pickup and roared out in a cloud of dust. Some of his hastily packed stuff fell off the large pile in the truck's bed but he didn't stop to get it. Eighteen men jumped into five vehicles and raced after him.

Jayce turned to Tim as they watched them go. "It looks like it's over, my friend!"

Tim let out a big sigh. "Yes. Thank you! I owe everyone a lot. Especially you."

"That's what friends are for." They smiled, shook hands, and used their free arms to complete back-thumping man-hugs.

Tim left to pick up his family and take them home. He couldn't wait to tell Evelyn the good news.

✳ ✳ ✳

When Burdett crossed the state line, the men in the other cars turned and headed home. A few miles down the highway Burdett stopped in a small clearing in the woods to take a leak. He was trembling with fury for being run out of town. He muttered as he emptied his bladder, "I'm going to kill that whole damn family and I'm going to love every minute of it! I'll make them pay in pain!" He laughed maniacally and got back in his truck.

* * *

Two hours later, state trooper Moe Ingram needed to relieve himself. He stopped in a clearing a bit off the highway in the woods. It was sometimes used as a love nest for teenagers, and he liked to check it out on his rounds. He remembered an incident at this site many years ago when his training officer and he had come across a bouncing car with windows fogged over. Officer Ingram had started to walk up to the car to break it up, but his trainer tapped him on the shoulder and whispered, "Not yet." The older cop then sneaked to the back of the car and laid his hand on the bumper, then whispered, "Not yet ... not yet ... NOW!"

They each rushed to a side of the car and banged on a door. Moe chuckled at the memories of the sights and sounds that followed, and those teen lovers' embarrassment. *If looks could kill, that young man would have been guilty of two murders that night!*

He noticed a beat-up yellow pickup on the edge of the clearing. Ingram shined his light on the plate and called it in. The response made him reach for his gun, call for backup, and approach the vehicle very carefully. He always did when suspects were as dangerous as William Burdett's rap sheet indicated he was.

He froze. What was left of Burdett's head dangled out the driver's side window frame. Blood was everywhere. The trooper flashed his light inside the truck and saw a very dead William Burdett with a gun clutched in his right hand. He sighed. *Another suicide. At least the world is better off with this one gone.* Just to be sure, he looked for fresh tire tracks and footprints. He caught a break. It had rained the night before, washing away older tracks and prints so new ones would be easy to spot. He found none. *Yep, suicide.*

Seventy-five miles away, Jayce Kendall's brain roiled. He'd followed the caravan and had caught up to it well before the border. The men in the trailing vehicles focused on the yellow pickup in front of them and didn't notice he'd followed several cars behind them. He pulled to the left of an eighteen-wheeler and kept going when the others exited to the right to head home. Burdett saw the others turn back, but, having never seen Jayce's car, he had no idea he was still being followed.

When Burdett pulled into the clearing in the woods, Jayce drove a little further down the road, pulled his car into the woods, cut his lights, and back-tracked on foot. Kendall knew Burdett would never leave his friends alone. The psychopath unknowingly sealed his fate when he heard Burdett vowing to kill them. Jayce had waited until Burdett had climbed back behind the steering wheel and then crept to the open window on the passenger side of the old yellow truck.

Burdett saw him and growled, "You! You're dead!"

He lunged for his gun under the seat.

"Looking for this?" When Burdett looked up, Jayce quickly leaned in, pressed the muzzle of Burdett's gun against the man's temple, and fired. It was the only way he could be sure Burdett would never have another "misunderstanding" with Tim and his family, or anyone else, again.

Jayce was pretty confident that when the police saw Burdett's rap sheet they wouldn't bother to investigate the obvious "suicide," but he decided to help them see wanted he wanted them to see.

He wiped his prints from the gun and placed it in Burdett's hand to make sure the psychopath's prints were where they needed to be. He arranged Burdett's hand and gun to make it look like he'd shot himself. The dead man's right hand had almost reached the gun when Jayce fired. It had been so close that cordite would settle on it, as it would have if Burdett himself had pulled the trigger. *Thank you for helping me to make it convincing, Burdett. I told you I was the man who would stop you from hurting my friend and his family. You should have listened.* Jayce shook his head as he took a big breath. *You bastard! It should never have come to this. I didn't want to kill you, but you gave me no choice!*

Jayce used a branch covered in leaves to wipe away his footprints. His gloves and long-sleeved shirt were spattered with blood. Before touching his car, he took off his gloves, turning them inside out. Jayce put the gloves into a plastic bag. He repeated the process with his shirt. It was fairly new and machine wash-able, so it had no identifying dry cleaner's marks on it. He sealed the bag and put it under his seat so it would be out of sight. His T-shirt was no match for the cold night air so he grabbed his jacket and put it on. He was grateful that he'd thought to leave his jacket in the car for the brief time he'd left his car. It was cold, but not so cold he couldn't go several minutes without it.

Jayce didn't want the recently-broken branch he'd used to cover his tracks at the crime scene to raise suspicion, so he put it on the passenger's seat. Four exits up the highway, when no other car was in sight he stopped on a small side road just long enough to throw the branch into the woods.

About halfway home, Jayce pulled into the parking lot of a fast food joint, parked, put on his jacket over his T-shirt and zipped it up. He went into the restroom, locked the door, quickly rinsed his hair, scrubbed his hands and all exposed skin with hot soapy water, and dried everything with the restroom's hot air blower. Jayce then bought a big meal to go. He ate it in his car, took his gloves and shirt out of the plastic bag and stuffed them in the large empty paper bag his meal had come in. He put the rest of the trash on top of the gloves and shirt, rolled the top closed, and threw it into the restaurant's half-full garbage can before leaving the parking lot. Because the plastic bag had traces of Burdett's blood on the inside and Jayce's fingerprints on the outside, he burned it in a fire pit in his back yard after he was sure his wife was asleep.

As Jayce lay on his back in bed, fingers interlaced between his head and pillow, he thought about what he'd done. He'd never killed a man before. He explored how he felt about it and was somewhat surprised at what he discovered. *If I'd killed almost any other man I'd feel terrible and remorseful. Ashamed. Perhaps even sick. But I don't feel any of that. Why not? Am I proud of what I've done? No. But, I feel no shame either.* A possible answer came to him. *Burdett* needed *killing. He was like a rabid dog or rattlesnake, but more calculating and vicious. A menace to society. No, while those may all be good reasons, they weren't why I killed him. It was far more personal than that. Burdett was going back to kill my best friend and his family. If I'd let him live it's likely he'd be over there killing them right now. I just couldn't let that happen. I did what I had to do to save them.*

He knew no one could ever learn what he'd done. He alone would carry the secret for the rest of his days.

Jayce closed his eyes, rolled over in his bed, and fell asleep almost instantly. He slept peacefully.

The Patsy

The little man eagerly read the obituaries as he did every day. Many people read the obits, and for a variety of often fine, or at least understandable, reasons, but Eddie's reason wasn't fine. In fact, whatever reasons the others had, his was likely to be the worst of all.

From Eddie's perspective he merely helped to prove the truth in the old saying, "A fool and his money are soon parted." In Eddie's case, the "fools" were not just anyone, but lonely, widowed, little old ladies who had no living next of kin and likely received a sizable life insurance payout on their recently deceased husbands. The older, weaker, and more desperate they were, the easier it was for Eddie. They were ripe for the picking. Eddie believed no one on the planet was a better picker of *that* fruit than himself. His string of successes stretched back many years and left in its wake more than fifty despondent and destitute elderly women.

It was all a game to him, and he fancied himself the master of it. The game proved quite lucrative. He enjoyed the money, but he loved even more seeing the look in the old ladies' eyes when they realized how foolish they'd been, how weak they were because they couldn't stop him, and how much bleaker their future had just become.

That look always reminded him of how he felt when his mother had rejected and abandoned him when he needed her the most. He preferred to believe that's what happened rather than face up to the truth: he'd lied to and stolen from her to such an extent that, by the time she'd finally stood up to him and told him "no," she had nothing left to lose. That didn't stop Eddie from taking out his anger and frustration on her. After having crippled her financially, he punched her in the face. Eddie then walked out of his mother's life forever. He smiled at the memory.

At least my old man was strong. He taught me about life and how to treat weaklings. Father knew how to live. He had freedom! Eddie remembered with pride how his father made sure his mother stayed afraid of him. *If she got out of line, he'd threaten her. If that didn't work, he'd deck her. After a while he didn't bother to make the threats and just punched her without warning. That kept her in line and let him do as he pleased.*

Thanks, old man, for teaching me to take what I want from the weak. It's smarter and safer that way. Eddie first had to learn that lesson the hard way. His father and older brother bullied him without mercy. They taunted—"This is what happens to weak little boys,"—and drilled it into his head with punches and kicks. Eddie learned the small and weak always paid a price. That was just the way of the world.

At first Eddie counted on his mother to protect him from them. After all, a mother was supposed to protect her children. She tried, again and again, but had been too small and weak to stop them. He hated her for that, and the hate turned to rage and fury. Now, any time he saw a vulnerable woman, he wanted to use and hurt her the way his mother had been used and had let him be hurt. Now he made sure that women paid for their weakness.

It was the only thing that ever made him feel strong.

Eddie had learned long ago not to bother with wealthy women. They often had advisors who could help them to avoid scammers and the types of "investment opportunities" he offered.

Eddie's targets of choice possessed little experience with large amounts of money and often knew nothing about investing or investments. They typically had no idea as to what to do with a $50,000 or $100,000 life insurance check. That's where Eddie came in. He had all kinds of ideas about what they could do with the money, ideas that filled Eddie's pockets.

Ideally, his targets faced large debts and/or feared outliving their money. Eddie knew desperate people were often the easiest to fool, because they so craved a silver bullet to make all their troubles go away. They *wanted* to believe, *needed* to believe. Without hope, people took chances on and clung to the flimsiest stories and most unlikely odds. Casinos, lotteries, and con men dangled hope, and desperate people reached for salvation, becoming unwitting puppets on their strings.

There! Faith Hansen. Faith. I love it. Even her name screams "Sucker!" I saw that name on one of the latest lists.

Over time, Eddie found and nurtured relationships with three low-paid employees working in different life insurance sales offices. He paid them to provide him with lists of people who had recently died, the amounts of life insurance paid out, their primary beneficiaries, their ages, addresses, and contact information.

Eddie told them he was a salesperson for mortuaries and cemeteries and bribed those gullible clerical workers with modest amounts of money to give them incentive. Hiding his true intent, he took all the names—not just those leaving behind grieving widows—and only used the ones he thought would make the best targets.

Eddie shuffled some papers and smiled with predatory greed. *"Ah, there it is! A $75,000 life insurance payout. The obit says her husband had been a manager of a small local hardware store. They outlived two children. Based on her poor dead husband's age, I'll bet she's about 85. Perfect!*

Eddie parked his nondescript car on Faith Hansen's quiet street, a few doors down from her modest home and waited until dusk. When no one was around, he hid between a couple of large bushes near her house. He pulled his shirt half out of his pants, ripped a sleeve, and yanked off the top two buttons. *Now for the part that's gonna get me in her door and make her feel sorry for me.* He held his palm about eighteen inches from his face. *This is my least favorite part of this version of the game.* He closed his eyes and

thrust his palm against his nose. *God that hurts!* Blood spewed
and he let it flow. It dripped over his lips and chin, down his neck,
and onto his white shirt. He smeared some on his hand. *Now I'm
ready.*

Eddie walked to his target's front door and rang the doorbell.
He imagined her putting down whatever book she was reading or
turning off the television, and wondering who it might be. The
porch light came on. A sweet-looking little old lady opened her
door, looked at the hurt man, and exclaimed, "Oh, my goodness!"

"I'm sorry, ma'am. I was walking by and saw three men who
appeared to be trying to steal your car. I tried to stop them,
and—"

"Oh you poor dear! Please, come in!" She let him in, closed
the door behind him, and led him toward the dining room. Eddie looked around the woman's modest, tidy home. The furniture
looked well taken care of, though far from new. Family photos
hung on the walls. A wedding photo showed two smiling young
people; it appeared to be several decades old. She'd been a beautiful blonde bride. He noticed she still wore her wedding ring.

"Please have a seat at the table, and I'll get something to help
stop the bleeding."

"No need to bother, ma'am. I'm sure I'll be fine. I just wanted
to warn you to be careful and watch out for them in case they
come back."

"Nonsense, young man! You sit right there and I'll be right
back." Her voice assumed a false sternness, but the sparkle in her
eyes and her warm smile assured him he was in good and caring
hands.

She returned with three towels, and handed the first to him.
"Here. An ice pack's inside. Tilt your head back and hold this
against your nose."

He did as he was told and winced at the pain. She handed a
second towel to him, wet and warm. "You can use this to clean the
blood off the rest of you, and here's another to dry yourself off."

When the blood stopped flowing, she offered, "There's a mirror in the bathroom, if that would be easier for you to clean up."

"Yes, please. That would be great."

She pointed down the hallway. "First door on the right."

"Thank you."

Eddie cleaned himself up and made sure to rinse and then wring out the towels with cold water. *It's what a thoughtful man would do. This is almost too easy.*

He brought the towels out and, assuming a sheepish demeanor, said, "I'm sorry. I soaked and rinsed these towels but couldn't get all the red out. Where may I put these?"

"I'll take them. Please, have a seat on the couch, young man, and I'll be right back." She took the towels out of the room and quickly returned. "It occurred to me that I don't even know your name. I'm Faith Hansen."

She held out her hand.

He stood and gently shook it. "I'm Owen Brewster."

"Thank you for courageously taking on three men to keep my car from being stolen!"

Giving his best "Aw, shucks, it weren't nothing, ma'am" look, Eddie said, "I'm just happy I was able to help."

He looked around again at her home. A look of grief washed over his face. Small tears began to pool on his lower eyelashes.

"Are you all right, Mr. Brewster?"

"I'm sorry. I saw your wedding picture and it made me think of Mary. We were married for fourteen years. She had cancer. We used every penny we had trying to help her get better. She seemed to beat it twice, but I lost her three months ago."

"I'm so sorry for your loss. I just lost my Stanley after forty-nine years of marriage."

"I'm sorry, I didn't know. You have my sincerest condolences, Mrs. Hansen." He looked around her living room again, as though examining the family photos, and more tears began to form. "I hope your home is safe. I'm about to lose mine. Oh, I'm sorry, I shouldn't burden you with my troubles when you surely have enough of your own."

"Nonsense, young man. I've learned it can help to talk about it. Please continue."

Eddie affected a sob. "We poured every penny into keeping Mary alive and got further and further behind on our house payment and property taxes. The bank was about a month away from taking away our home. Somebody who I thought was a friend offered to give me $70,000 to pay off the entire remaining loan and the back taxes if I would sign a note giving half the equity in the house to him. Under the circumstances, his offer seemed better than losing the house and all the money I put into it for all those years. I accepted his offer, but instead of getting the money to me, he made excuse after excuse about why it would be just a bit longer before he could get the money. The bank foreclosed. My 'friend' then laughed in my face and said, 'I decided to just buy your house at the auction. I researched it and found I'll very likely win with a $70,000 bid. Then I'll have all the equity and not just half.'"

"That's a terrible thing to do to you!"

"Yes, I felt so hurt and betrayed. I trusted him, and now he's going to steal the home that Mary and I had lived in for all those years. If only I could find a way to come up with $75,000 cash by tomorrow. I'd gladly give half the equity in my home to anyone who could help me buy it back at the auction. I'd immediately sell the house. I talked to two Realtors and they both assured me that it's worth at least $325,000. Whoever put up the $75,000 could easily double their money in a month or two, but I don't know anyone who has that kind of money."

"Well, Mr. Brewster—"

"Please, call me Owen."

"Thank you, Owen. My goodness, our oldest son was named Owen. I don't hear that name very often." A wistful look darkened her face for a moment. "Our dear Owen died in a car crash. He was only forty-five."

"I'm awfully sorry to hear that, Mrs. Hansen. It must have been a terrible loss for you and Mr. Hansen. "

She slowly nodded, as her eyes misted over. She blinked a couple of times and looked at him. "Please call me Faith."

"Thank you, Faith. Did you say your son was forty-five? I just turned forty-five in May."

She shook her head at the serendipity of it all and appeared to come to a decision. "You could be the answer to my prayers. It just so happens that the life insurance money I received after Stanley died is just sitting in my savings account. I need that $75,000 to pay off a balloon loan coming due in three months. We got the life insurance policy for that amount when we took out the balloon loan ten years ago, just in case anything happened to my husband or our savings. Treating my husband's illness used up nearly all of our savings. If I don't pay off the loan, I could lose my house. But if I do pay it off, my savings will run out in a few years even if I stay healthy. And if I get sick—"

Her voice faded, and she blinked a few times to ward off tears. "So, you see, maybe our meeting and your situation is a sign from God."

"Oh, Mrs. Hans—uh, Faith, I couldn't possibly impose on you in this way. You barely know me and—"

"You didn't know me at all, and yet you just fought three men to save me from having my car stolen. That tells me a lot about the kind of man you are. Please let me return the favor. Besides, doubling my money within sixty days would help me to pay off that balloon loan and provide me with $75,000 to live on. I may need it. My mother and grandmother both lived to be at least 95 years old."

"I guess those are all good points, Faith. Okay, you've convinced me. The auction is at noon tomorrow and because they've received some forged cashier's checks lately, they now only accept cash. How about I draw up an agreement giving you half the equity from the sale of my house, and you have the cash ready when I come by here tomorrow at 10 am? Can you get that much cash so quickly? I know banks tend not to let go of it that fast."

Faith thought for a moment, "I know a way to do it. Okay, partner. We won't let your so-called 'friend' get away with stealing your house from you." She smiled sweetly.

"It's a deal! See you tomorrow morning at ten."

Driving home, Eddie smiled at his good fortune. *With that balloon loan hanging over her head and almost no other savings, she's desperate.* He loved working with desperate people.

On the drive back to his latest victim's home the next morning, Eddie gloated to himself. *These lonely little old ladies are such patsies.* He smiled to himself over his cleverness and how foolish they all were. *They're all the same. Flash a smile, get them to trust you, talk them into giving their life savings to you in cash, and then split.*

He'd already bilked three little old ladies in the last six weeks, and anticipated taking every penny this old crone had. *"It's almost like shooting fish in a barrel, only easier. After this job I'll have enough money to finally take an around-the-world cruise and not come back for a year.*

Over the years, Eddie had perfected his "I'm an honest and helpful man" facial expressions. He altered the way he began each scam, so the cops and little old ladies wouldn't get wise and to make the game even more interesting for him. He'd never tried the "I fought three men to save your car" act before, but it had worked like a charm.

He found that the most trustworthy women were the easiest to trick, especially if they were afraid their money would run out and were desperate to find ways to grow what savings they had left. Trust and fear made a potent combination. Augmented by his silver-tongued talents, they worked like magic. Plus, he always had a back-up plan. If his victims showed the cash to him and then tried to back out, he simply bashed them, locked them in a closet with the back of a chair jammed under the door knob, grabbed their life's savings, and ran. What did he care if no one found them for days? That just gave him more time to get away clean.

Despite his small stature, Eddie still stood nearly a foot taller than his new victim. He carefully selected every item of his clothing to give the impression that he was humble, modest, hardworking, and most importantly, trustworthy. He needed his image to broadcast, "You can trust me." The rolled-up sleeves of his light blue shirt hinted at how hard working he was. Its wrinkled fabric reminded his victim that his alleged wife had died and to indicate that ironing wasn't high on this widowers to-do list. His jeans were basic, clean, without holes, and held up by a simple and inexpensive brown leather belt. His polished leather shoes showed wear at the heels.

So giddy at what he was about to do to the old lady, the con man almost skipped to Faith's front door. *Now comes my reward and her ruin. It doesn't get any better than this.* He thought back to his own "dear" mother and the way she had disowned him. He conveniently ignored the fact that he'd punched her so hard when she finally refused to give him the last of her money that she'd been hospitalized for two weeks. He smiled inwardly as he rang the doorbell.

Faith opened the door with that sweet, innocent, smile he so detested. Eddie flashed his best, trust-inspiring smile right back at her.

"You're right on time, young man. I appreciate punctuality. Please come in." She motioned him to the dining room table. "Have a seat. Would you like some lemonade?"

"That's kind, but no thank you." Eddie reached into his pocket and pulled out the one-page document he'd typed, clearly spelling out the terms of their arrangement. "Please me know if you have any questions."

Eddie noticed that Faith's hands were shaking as she read it. *Uh oh. She might be getting cold feet. It's one thing to talk about entrusting nearly every penny one has to a stranger, but it's never quite so easy to actually do it. Well, I've seen all this before and know how to deal with it.*

Faith finished reading the agreement and carefully set it on the table. It was exactly as they'd agreed to the evening before. At the bottom of the page were lines for their signatures, dates, and printed names. She saw that he'd already signed and filled in his other two lines.

Eddie asked, "Do you have any questions?"

"No. It seems clear and as we agreed."

"Glad to hear it." Eddie placed a pen on the page. "By the way, where's the cash?"

She pointed to a large cloth bag sitting next to her chair. Stuffed to the brim, it bulged at the seams.

"Did the bank give you any trouble getting that much cash?"

Faith smiled and leaned toward him. She spoke softly and in a conspiratorial manner. "It wasn't in a bank. My husband and I were youngsters during the Great Depression. We saw what happened to our parents and neighbors when so many banks failed. They didn't have FIDC back then. We never forgot that lesson, and until now never had much money to worry about anyway, so I cashed the insurance check and gradually moved it all into cash. It took several trips to the bank to do it, but I felt safer with it at home with me. I know it might seem silly to a young man such as you, Eddie, but old habits and fears die hard when you reach my age." She looked at the clock. "When should we leave for the auction?"

Her words alarmed Eddie. "Wait a minute. You're not planning to come to the auction with me, are you, Faith? That would be very unsafe for you. I've heard stories that, with people carrying so much cash at the auctions, it's not unusual for bad guys to mug and rob innocent folks. I wouldn't want you to get hurt or be robbed."

"But there is safety in numbers. Wouldn't it be safer for two people to go, rather than one?" Her voice wavered. "It's all the money I have."

"I understand. I really do, but I couldn't forgive myself if you got hurt trying to help me with my problem. I just fought three men to protect your car. I promise to protect your money with my life. It'll be safe." He motioned for her to hand the bag to him.

With some difficulty Faith lifted the heavy bag and stood up. She could barely hold it. Her hands shook, but not from the weight. With a trembling voice, Faith spoke so softly it was almost a whisper. "But this is all I have. I don't know what I'd do if I lost it."

Eddie couldn't tell whether she was talking to herself or to him, nor did he care. He sought to reassure her. "There's nothing to worry about, Faith. I'll come back right after the auction and add your name to the deed. You can keep the deed until my house sells and bring it to the escrow office yourself. That's how much I trust you."

"Well, that does make me feel a little better. Since you are such a nice man, I guess it's safe."

Eddie smiled with a mouth full of sparkling white teeth. "You won't regret this."

She held out the full bag. He put his hands on it, but she wouldn't let go. "I still want to go to the auction with you."

He tugged firmly, so firmly that she rose onto the tips of her toes and tilted toward him, still holding onto the bag.

Eddie's countenance changed. A threatening look replaced the smile. "Give me that bag!"

He ripped it from her hands and reveled in the shocked and fearful look on her face.

"Please, no!"

"Shut up old lady. I tried doing it the easy way, but you just *had* to fight me." He slung the bag over his shoulder and grabbed her wrist, yanking her toward the nearest bedroom, and looking for a closet to cage the crone.

She begged, "Please, you're hurting me!"

"Good! Shut up or you'll get worse than that. In fact, now that you've pissed me off, I'm going to leave you with something to remember me by."

The first bedroom he found had a closet door with the type of doorknob suitable for jamming a chair under. He smiled at the thought of hurting her some more as he turned the doorknob and yanked open the door. His smile vanished as he looked inside and a huge fist smashed into his still-sore nose. The large, muscular man attached to the huge fist followed up the first devastating blow with an even harder one to Eddie's mouth that split both lips and knocked out his two front teeth. The little man crumpled like the paper tiger he'd always been.

* * *

When the bloody con man came to, his skinny hands had been threaded through slats of the back of the chair in which he now sat. Handcuffs bound his wrists behind the chair. Judging by the pain in his wrists, he'd been cuffed none too gently and for quite a while. He tried moving his arms to no avail. It was clear he wasn't going anywhere. Even his body weight worked against him as he sat on the chair.

The big man watched him come to and try to move his hands. He laughed. "Go ahead, little man. Try to escape. Nothing would give me greater pleasure right now than to have you try."

Then he read the Miranda warning to him. "We finally caught you, Eddie, thanks to my grandmother." He nodded to Faith and beamed with pride. "Grandpa would have been so proud of you!"

"How do you know my name?" Eddie mumbled through swollen, split lips.

"I found your wallet and ran your ID."

Eddie hung his head. Blood from the two blows he received soaked his clothes.

The muscular man laughed again. "Don't worry about your clothes. You'll soon be getting a clean, new set provided by the state that you'll be wearing for a long, long time. To ensure that they give you the welcome you deserve, we're going to spread the word inside about how you like to hurt little old ladies. I'm pretty sure they other inmates will be thinking about their own loving grandmas when they roll out the red carpet for you." He added with a menacing growl, "You better not let a drop of blood get on any of my grandmother's furniture or carpet. Understand?"

The smaller man's eyes grew wide as he nodded his head. He winced at the pain that bobbing his head caused and felt around with his tongue to confirm the absence of his two front teeth. He soon also realized he'd peed himself.

"Grandma, do you have anything you'd like to say to this fine specimen of deficient and malignant humanity?"

She smiled at his use of such words, one of the many benefits of his solid college education. "Yes, Stanley, I would."

He winced at her use of his full first name in front of Eddie. She was the only one who called him Stanley. He was Stan to everyone else. Faith made a mental note to refrain from calling him Stanley in front of others.

She turned to the bloody little man and said, "Eddie, I'm very pleased and proud to introduce my grandson, Detective Stan Harris." She glanced at her grandson and smiled, then looked back at the creep. "There is nothing lower than people like you who hurt others just for the fun of it. Two months ago you stole every penny my best friend Nancy Carlton had: all fifty thousand dollars of the life insurance money she received from her recently deceased husband's policy. You devastated her financially. With such a bleak future, she lost the will to live and nearly died because of you. That's when I swore I'd do whatever it took to turn the tables on you and put you away for so long you'll never again be able to hurt another grieving widow."

"It was Grandma's idea to create the false obituary using a phony last name. You had so many victims, that we had a pretty good idea as to your perfect target. You fell for Grandma's trap hook, line, and sinker." The detective looked at the small woman with a look of such pride that she blushed. "By the way, Grandma, I forgot to mention that there's a $50,000 reward for the capture of this slime ball, and you've earned it."

She beamed at the surprising news. "That's wonderful! I'll be able to give Nancy the amount this … this 'slime ball' stole from her."

Faith walked over and stood in front of the little man. She stared into his eyes for a minute, trying unsuccessfully to find even the slightest trace of humanity in his eyes. Then her eyes grew wide. "Oh, my God! I knew your mother, Eddie."

The statement shocked the detective. "What? How?" Eddie just stared at her.

"Things started falling into place when I heard your real name, and I just now put it together. I volunteered at a women's shelter. One day a woman with your last name came in after spending two weeks in the hospital. She had three fractures in her face and a black eye. During her stay at the shelter, I learned her adult son named Eddie smashed her face when she had no more money to give to him. To give to *you*! You took it all and abandoned her."

Eddie stared at Faith and said, "So what? She deserved it!"

"You never visited her in the hospital, never checked to see how she was doing. She died shortly after, I think more from a broken heart than anything else."

Eddie's words dripped like bloody daggers, "Isn't that just too bad?"

"Your mother forgave you, Eddie. She said your father turned you into what you became, and that you'd once been a sweet little boy. She never stopped loving you."

Eddie opened his mouth to speak, but no words came out. She saw the shock and surprise in his eyes at her message. For the first time, she looked at him with pity.

No one said anything for quite a while. Then the detective looked at the broken little man and said, "Eddie, I want to show you something."

Stan pulled some small recording devices and tiny cameras from his pockets and laid them on the table in front of the de-fanged predator. He flipped a switch. Eddie groaned when he heard his voice threaten Faith and her cry of pain. Stan said, "I collected these from the dining room and bedroom while you were, uh, indisposed, and checked to make sure we captured your entire performance. We got it all. You're the star of your own show, but somehow I doubt anyone on the jury is going to be asking you for autographs."

Someone knocked on the front door. Faith answered it and invited a uniformed policewoman into the house. The officer saw the damage to the perpetrator and said to the detective, "I see this perp must have attacked your grandmother and resisted arrest."

"Yes. I believe he prefers to pick on innocent elderly ladies rather than people who are more able to defend themselves. I read his rights to him. Please take this cowardly rat and put him in a cage."

"It'll be my pleasure."

Faith looked up at her handsome grandson and asked, "Well, Stanley, how'd I do?"

With a warm smile carefully wrapped the tiny lady in his muscular arms. "You did great, Grandma. You should have been an actress. You helped save other vulnerable widows from this creep. I'm proud of you."

With a twinkle in her eyes and a beaming smile, she said, "That was fun. Can we do it again sometime?"

About the Author

Russ Towne lives with his wife in Campbell, California, USA. They've been married since 1979; have three adult children, and five grandchildren. His passions include family, friends, writing and investing. Russ wrote his first book in 2013 when he was fifty-six and has written and published dozens of books that can be found on Amazon.com and elsewhere.

Russ savors experiencing nature, especially near rivers and streams that run through giant redwood groves, and near beautiful beaches. He enjoys watching classic movies, reading, and his tiny fern garden and redwood grove. Russ greatly enjoys managing the investments of Clients of the wealth management firm he founded in 2003.

Amazon Author's Page
https://www.amazon.com/author/russtowne.

Blog: Russ Towne's A Grateful Man
http://russtowne.com

The titles of the books he has written, compiled, and published include:

FICTION

It Was Her Eyes

NOVELLA

Touched
Short Stories and Flash Fiction

Palpable Imaginings
An Anthology of Stories by Several Writers in Various Genres.

NON-FICTION

Honest, Honey, That's How It Happened

Stop Peeing in the Kitty Litter!

Slices of Life
An Anthology of the Selected Nonfiction Stories of Several Writers.

Reflections from the Heart of a Grateful Man

BOOKS FOR YOUNG CHILDREN:

Sunny Saves the Day

Mysti Z's Magical Day

Wilbur the Duck Who Flew Upside Down

Sir Alex Sleighs a Dragon

Flora Belle and Dreami Dragon

The Beach that Love Built

A Day in the Shade of a Tickletoe Tree

Zach and the Toad Who Rode a Bull

V. G. and Dexter Dufflebee

Ki-Gra's REALLY, REALLY BIG Day!
Clyde and Friends
Clyde and Hoozy Whatzadingle
Clyde and I Help a Hippo to Fly
Rusty Bear and Thomas, Too
Clyde and I

POETRY

Kaleidoscope

Heart Whispers
An Anthology of the Selected Works of Over 20 Poets.

Made in the USA
Columbia, SC
13 June 2018